DEEPER THAN LOVE

DELANEY DIAMOND

GARDEN AVENUE PRESS

Deeper Than Love by Delaney Diamond

Copyright © 2019, Delaney Diamond

Garden Avenue Press

Atlanta, Georgia

ISBN: 978-1-946302-10-6 (Ebook edition)

ISBN: 978-1-946302-11-3 (Paperback edition)

www.delaneydiamond.com

CHAPTER 1

$\mathcal{R}$eese exited the shower, rubbing a towel vigorously over his damp hair and padding naked across the cool tile and onto the thick, sumptuous carpet in the bedroom of the hotel suite. Casting his eyes around, he searched for his shirt and pants in the piles of clothes strewn across the floor and on top of the armchair near the window.

Chelsea, one of the two young women in the bed, rolled in his direction, her dark brown skin making a striking contrast against the starkness of the white sheets. She brushed long hair out of her face and squinted at him.

"You're leaving?" Her hoarse voice was filled with disappointment.

Reese nodded. "Afraid so. Much as I'd like to stick around, I've got to get out of here. It's almost noon, and I have plans." He didn't have plans. He was just ready to go after a long night and late morning.

He tossed the damp towel on a chair by the window and pulled on his underwear, a pair of washed-out jeans, and the dress shirt he'd worn the night before to a party that started in one of the other suites. After lots of flirting, he'd booked a room for Chelsea and her brunette friend, who was still fast asleep on the other pillow, one lovely breast and nipple revealed by the lowered linens. It had been a good night indeed.

He sat on the end of the bed and started putting on his shoes. Chelsea crawled over and draped an arm over his shoulder.

"When will I see you again?"

"Not for a while. You go back to New York tomorrow, don't you?"

He met her at a friend's book launch and signing, and they hooked up that night. From their conversation the next day, it was a revenge tactic against her on-again/off-again boyfriend, with whom she was currently off. When they spotted each other at last night's party, she'd told him she and her boyfriend were done for good and had been more than willing to take another tumble in the sheets. He'd been pleasantly surprised when she invited a friend along.

"I do. When are you back in New York?" she asked.

"Don't know. But when I am, I'll be sure to call you." Reese stood and rolled up his shirtsleeves to his elbows. "The two of you are welcome to stay as long as you like. Have lunch on me before you leave. Good seeing you again."

She pouted, but he ignored her and patted his pants pockets to make sure he had his wallet and phone and headed toward the door.

"Bye. See you next time," she called.

He didn't respond because he didn't know if there really would be a next time. Having sex was not the same as starting a relationship, and unless they ran into each other again, he wouldn't call her and was fairly certain she wouldn't call him, either. In the end, the way their night ended suited them both just fine.

Reese took the elevator to the first floor and walked over to the registration desk. After waiting in line for a few minutes, he approached the young woman behind the counter.

He gave her the suite number and added, "I have two guests who are still in the room. They can stay as long as they need to, and anything they want can be billed to the card on file."

"No problem, Mr. Brooks. Did you enjoy your stay?"

"It was excellent," he said, flashing his first smile of the morning.

"We do hope you'll join us again," she said, blushing and lowering her gaze.

"I'm sure I will."

He walked away and stepped onto the sidewalk, squinting into the glare of the summer sun. He pulled out his phone to call a car when a flash of yellow and blue down the street at The Winthrop Hotel caught his eye, but the woman disappeared behind a column.

He gaped when she reappeared. Were his eyes deceiving him? No. It was Nina Winthrop. His girl was back. His baby. He'd missed her like crazy. The bright day suddenly became brighter.

She entered the hotel, and Reese took off through the stream of cars that packed the road. Drivers irritably honked their horns as he wound in between the vehicles, focused on getting to her.

"Sorry," he said, lifting a conciliatory hand but not slowing down.

Reese flew past the doorman and rushed into the cavernous foyer. He spotted Nina standing in the middle of the tiled floor and rushed over to where she stood, staring down at her phone with an embroidered bag over one shoulder. He intended to grab her from behind but never got that far. A tall white man in a suit, who he hadn't noticed because he only had eyes for her, stepped between them and shoved Reese hard, forcing him to stumble backward.

"Son of a…" Startled, Reese stared up at the giant.

3

"Stand back," the bigger man said in a stern voice, his eyes narrowing.

Nina stepped around the burly bodyguard, and when she saw Reese, she placed a calming hand on the big man's arm. "Stan, it's all right. I know him."

As Stan eased out of the way, Reese glared at him. Then he focused his attention on Nina. Too long had passed since he'd seen her in the flesh, and she looked better than any photo or video she'd shared over the past few years.

With a wide grin, he rushed over and swooped her into his arms.

"Reese!" Her surprised laughter swept into his ears.

Goosebumps broke out on his skin. He loved the way she said his name—even when she was angry and turned it into two syllables by placing emphasis on the first e.

He squeezed her tight and kissed her cheek, reveling in the achingly sweet scent of her skin. She smelled so good. Familiar and sweet.

He set her back on her feet and took inventory of her appearance. She wore a blue and yellow halter-topped sundress that exposed her back and shoulders and a matching head wrap. Thick gold hoops hung from her ears, and a nose stud glinted in her left nostril.

"Damn, you look good."

He'd forgotten how beautiful she was. The fullness of her lips, the ripe curves of her sexy frame, and the husky sound of her voice. Did he really forget, or was it that he didn't want to remember because he would miss her so much he'd get on a plane to wherever she was in the world? He should have.

"Thanks. You look great, too," she said softly.

"Why didn't you tell me you were back?"

"If I'd known I'd get such an enthusiastic greeting, I would have called you right away."

He took a good look at her bright eyes and smiling face. "You should've called me right away anyway, but I forgive you."

"Now I can sleep better tonight," Nina said.

Reese chuckled. "It's been too long," he said in a low voice, biting his bottom lip.

Nina had glowing chestnut-brown skin, long thick lashes, and the prettiest, sexiest rosebud mouth any woman had ever been blessed with. She was so damn beautiful, she looked like a doll—completely unreal. The crazy thing about Nina was that she didn't even try, and when she told him she was going to become a nomad and travel around the world, he'd been worried about all the men she'd meet who would certainly fall for her stellar looks and great personality.

On more than one occasion he'd been tempted to join her overseas, but not only had she never invited him, he got the distinct impression that she'd wanted to be alone. And he understood. After her father died, he recognized that leaving was part of her process of healing.

The bodyguard was her mother's way of making sure that her daughter remained safe while traveling, but Nina hated having a shadow, and Stan's days were numbered now that they were stateside.

"So what are you going to do after the wedding? You going back on the road, or are you back for good?"

Her older sister Lindsay was getting married to his cousin Malik.

"I'm back for good."

That's what he hoped she'd say.

"Perfect," Reese said, wanting to hug her again. Now he'd have a chance to make up for lost time and correct the mistakes of the past. Dumb mistakes he'd made at nineteen years old— mistakes that to this day he still berated himself over.

She looked around. "What are you doing here at my hotel?"

5

"Actually, I went to a party at the Ritz last night and stayed overnight to…to sleep off my buzz. I saw you as I was leaving."

One of her eyebrows shot toward the edge of the head wrap. She knew him well enough to know that was a BS answer. "So, what's her name? Or their names?" she asked.

"There you go, thinking the worst of me, as usual."

"But I'm right, aren't I? I see nothing's changed."

It bothered him that she thought he remained unchanged when, in reality, he was simply killing time with other women until he won her back.

He moved on to another subject. "Soon as you get settled in, we need to get together and catch up. I want to know everything about your trip."

An expression of unease flitted across her face. "I don't know if I'll have a lot of time. I have a million things to take care of with The Winthrop Hotel Group. Next week I'm going into the office for meetings and—"

"Make time." A thread of tension surfaced between them. "You and I have unfinished business."

"I don't know what you're talking about."

"You know what I'm talking about. You gonna make me spell it out?" This wasn't how he'd anticipated their first meeting going upon her return, but he'd had enough of her running from him. They needed to address the issue head-on. "The kiss, Nina."

She made a big show of placing the phone in her large bag. "I already told you, it was nothing."

"It didn't feel like nothing."

"That kiss was a moment of weakness. I was emotional because it was the anniversary of my father's death." She faced him with defiance in her eyes, daring him to contradict her.

"I know you were hurting, but there was more than pain in that kiss," he said quietly.

He continued to be haunted by that night, the way her body

molded to his, the softness of her lips. To this day, he didn't know how he managed to control himself and simply offer comfort instead of indulging in the lust that raged inside him. He deserved an award for exhibiting such a Herculean act of restraint.

Even now, the urge to lift her in his arms and kiss the lies from her lips overtook him, but he silenced the beast within and exercised a level of patience he didn't usually display when he wanted something.

Reese prowled closer, and her body stiffened, but she didn't step back. He almost smiled at her stubbornness. That was the Nina he knew—defiant, proud, not willing to back down.

He bent his head to whisper in her ear and heard the shaky breath she took. "You can't keep running from me, Nina. One of these days, I'm going to catch you."

CHAPTER 2

*M*ina gritted her teeth to resist retreating from Reese's domineering presence. Why did he always have to look so fine? And smell good, too. He smelled clean and fresh, the subtle scent of soap indicating a recent shower. His Caesar haircut was pristine, and his jawline sharp and sturdy—very masculine.

Being held against his tall, fit body had been way too enjoyable. Lean muscles traversed from feet to neck, and whether he wore jeans or a suit, Reese always looked sexy in a way no man had a right to be. As if that weren't enough, he had the kind of voice that made panties drop. Literally. She'd dropped hers years ago, with him speaking only a few words in his low tenor and lighting her skin on fire with his touch.

The dusting of freckles across the bridge of his nose and cheeks were darker than usual on his fawn-colored skin because, in the summer, he spent a lot of time outdoors waterskiing and playing football. His lips, often turned up in a sexy smile that tempted with their fullness, sat firmly pressed together with a seriousness that matched the expression in his dark brown eyes.

After straightening the bag on her shoulder, Nina stated, "You don't get to dictate my time."

"I'm asking you to make time for me. You've been on this bullshit I'm-too-busy tip for three years now."

She bristled at his tone. "It's not bullshit. I *have* been busy."

Reese tilted his head to the side. "Not too busy to talk to your sister."

"You make it sound like you and I never communicated."

"Moments that were few and far between, and most of the time, I had to reach out."

Maybe that should give you a clue, Nina thought, but she refrained from saying the words out loud.

"We need to talk. Call me when you get settled."

He lightly touched her chin with two fingers, dusting heat over her skin. Internally, she shivered, hating herself for having such a profound reaction to his touch.

"If you don't, I'll come find you." Reese started toward the door.

"I'll call you when I have time," Nina yelled after him.

He continued walking out into the street as if she hadn't said a word. As if his word were law.

She muttered a curse under her breath and headed toward the elevator with Stan behind her.

Who did Reese think he was, anyway? She had important issues to worry about. She was the sole heir to her father's hotel empire and needed to figure out what type of role she would take on now that she was back in the States. Nothing on her to-do list included dealing with Reese and his sudden interest in her because of a kiss that took place over three years ago, a kiss she now regretted because ever since then, he'd become more aggressive in his attention.

That he wanted her back, she didn't doubt, but Reese's interest was purely sexual. She learned that harsh lesson when she gave him her virginity. Big mistake. She'd thought she was

9

special but knew better now. She was one of many, and that number had increased exponentially over the years.

Nina rode the elevator up to her apartment and stepped off with hard, hurried steps. Stan kept pace right behind her.

At the door to her apartment, she paused. "You can take off the rest of the day. I'll be fine," she told him.

His blond brows furrowed. "Are you sure about that, Miss Winthrop?"

She was younger than him and didn't feel like a "Miss Winthrop," but he had declined her request to call her Nina.

"Yes, I'm sure. Thank you, and I'll see you tomorrow around eight?"

Stan nodded and waited until she went inside.

Nina leaned back against the door and breathed a sigh of relief now that she was in her own space. The brief meeting with Reese had drained her.

She climbed the four steps that led into the open living room. From up here, she had an impressive view of the city, in a place filled with expensive mid-century-designed furnishings atop blonde wood floors. The sprawling apartment was over five thousand square feet and previously occupied by her father when he was alive. She inherited it, just like she did his business and assets.

Nina didn't have to work, and so far she hadn't since he passed away four and a half years ago—not traditionally, anyway. Not knowing what she would do with her life and how her future would unfold made her restless and apprehensive. People expected that she would take over her father's hotel business, but she wasn't sure it was something that she was capable of handling.

The whole idea of running a multimillion-dollar hotel empire was terribly intimidating, and she was more than happy to let the executives and Board of Directors continue their work. But her father had envisioned that she would take the reins one day and had arranged for two consultants to work with her. Instead, she'd started traveling the world.

Nina walked back to the master suite, and as she opened the door, the scent of a familiar perfume hit her nose. She broke out in a grin.

"Surprise!" Lindsay, her older half-sister, popped up from a chair by the window and flung her arms wide.

"Heyyy!"

They rushed into each other's arms. Nina squeezed her sister hard, needing a hug more than she realized. She and Lindsay had talked often while she traveled, and she'd been back a few times in the interim, but they were as close as two sisters could be, going so far as to having the same tattoo on their left biceps: *My sister is my best friend.* Having her here was the perfect welcome home.

Nina stepped back. "Is that my scarf?" she asked, pointing at the Ankara-print scarf Lindsay had tied around her head, with blonde braids peeping out the top in a secured bun.

"Yep. I went shopping in your closet while I waited. Don't I look fabulous?" Lindsay angled her head one way and then the other.

Nina was convinced there wasn't anything her sister couldn't wear. Lindsay was gorgeous, with hazel eyes and a complexion that was a shade lighter than Nina's.

"Yes, you look fabulous. Don't forget to return it, please."

She was actually teasing. They'd been borrowing each other's clothes and accessories for years, though nowadays it was mostly accessories. They were both busty women, but that's where the similarities in body shape ended. Her sister was tall and voluptuous, while Nina was shorter and slender.

Lindsay returned to the chair and crossed her long legs. "I told the front desk to let me know when you arrived. What took you so long to come up? I feel like I've been waiting forever."

Nina picked up one of the bags the bellhop had brought up earlier. "I got sidetracked. I ran into Reese downstairs."

"*Oh.* I bet that was interesting."

"That's an understatement," Nina muttered, taking the suitcase into the walk-in closet, a room almost the same size as the bedroom, with garments and shoes arranged on the shelves and racks in color-coordinated order.

"What happened?" Lindsay called out.

"He wants to talk." Nina returned to the room and plopped onto the bed.

"You knew that was coming."

"Yes, but not so soon. I just got back today."

"Did you tell him about Andy?"

Nina met Andy von Trapp on an organic farm in New Zealand, and they quickly connected, both surprised when they learned of their mutual ties to Atlanta. It was uncanny how in sync they were.

"It was hard to slip into the conversation. The timing wasn't right."

Seeing Reese had thrown her completely off guard. She'd been so unprepared for his appearance, she hadn't told him she was in a serious, committed relationship with another man.

"You better make time. You've had other boyfriends in the past, but since that kiss, Reese has changed. He's not going to take your new relationship well. I've told you before that he still has feelings for you."

"There you go again." Nina rolled her eyes.

"I'm not wrong. That kiss changed everything. Made him think he has a chance."

There was definitely some truth to her sister's words, all the more reason to stay away from him. Remaining friends with an ex presented its own set of challenges, and the kiss only complicated their relationship.

On the first anniversary of her father's death, Nina had

found comfort in his arms. They hadn't gone any further than kisses, but she recalled each one in vivid detail and regretted their hot and heavy make-out session. She'd enjoyed his touch way more than she should, which had reawakened feelings and desires that scared the hell out of her.

Lindsay jumped up from the chair and walked over to the bed. She took Nina's hand and pulled her up. "Listen, this is not the time for moping or being upset. The Winthrop sisters are back together. I'm getting married in two weeks, and you've found a man who you're a great match with. By the way, where is Andy?"

"In New York, visiting his dad. He'll be here next week."

"Great, so we have the whole weekend to spend time together and celebrate. Have you had lunch?"

"No, but now that you mention it, I'm starving." Nina patted her stomach.

"Perfect. Let's grab a bite to eat. On me." Lindsay headed for the door.

"Where are we going?" Nina asked, following.

"How about that salad place? I can't eat too much if I want to fit into my wedding dress. Can you believe I'm getting married?"

They walked down the stairs and out into the hallway. Nina hooked her arm through her sister's. "I definitely can. You're Lindsay, the Sexy Diva."

That was her moniker for a popular podcast on sex, dating, and relationships, which had turned into a book deal and launched a two-hour call-in radio show once a week.

Lindsay let out a throaty laugh. "Who knows, maybe we'll be planning a wedding for you, too soon," she said.

"That would be nice."

With regard to relationships, she and Reese were on the opposite end of the spectrum. True enough, they were practically kids when they had their love affair, but she was older and wiser now. Not the same naïve, foolish teenager she'd been when she fell for him.

Reese could push all he wanted, but she refused to fall under his spell again because she knew better. Not only could he not be trusted, but she wanted a husband and kids. Reese, on the other hand, didn't want to get married, and children were a no-go. That's why Andy was perfect for her. They were in sync about what they wanted out of marriage and life.

Nina glanced at her sister's smiling face. Lindsay appeared to be happier than she'd ever seen her, and Nina became a little jealous.

She'd be happier, too, if she hadn't run into Reese.

CHAPTER 3

*A*rms crossed, Nina turned in a slow circle in the middle of the office her father used to occupy. The two management consultants standing nearby didn't speak and allowed her to make the inspection in silence.

She'd spent the better part of the day walking through The Winthrop Hotel Group headquarters, greeting members of the staff, and reacquainting herself with the layout of the offices.

If she decided to move into this office and take over the role of CEO, there was some work to be done. Most of the furniture was gone from the room. Only a gray couch, a desk, and an executive chair remained. She would have to add her touches—her own desk and chair, perhaps group some sofas and a table over to the side to create a sitting area. On the walls, she'd place photos from her travels and awards she had received for her work in the community.

"What do you think?" Thomas asked.

He was the elder of the two consultants, with mahogany skin and his hair sprinkled with gray. As far as Nina was concerned, he was overdressed in a three-piece suit, but she had never seen him in anything less.

"It's a possibility," she said, scanning the large windows that took up two walls of the corner office.

They'd discussed moving her in here or finding another one in the building, but she wasn't sure what she would do.

"There's no rush," said the other woman in the room. Misha worked for the same firm but was younger than Thomas, with ivory skin and chestnut-colored hair. She always wore black glasses, a black suit, and her hair in a tight chignon, as if her entire look was a uniform.

"Don't worry, I'll take my time. I'll see you two on Monday?" Nina said.

"That's correct. We'll meet you in the conference room." Misha looked at Thomas for confirmation, and he nodded.

Nina smiled gratefully at them. They'd held her hand since she returned a week ago, and she trusted their advice. Her father had done well by hiring their firm to assist her in the transition to managing the company—assuming that's what she wanted to do.

"Good. I'll see you both before the Helping Hands presentation."

The Winthrop Helping Hands Program was an idea she'd tossed around with her father years ago, which she hoped to implement company-wide. The concept was very simple: pay employees to do volunteer work in their communities. It was for sure a radical premise, which over the past year had been rolled out among the east coast hotels.

The whole idea made her nervous because she knew what people called her behind her back—The Heir. The nickname was not a compliment. They saw her as useless, someone who got in the way and came up with ideas that created problems for staff, and it didn't help that she looked younger than her twenty-nine years. The purposely cruel nickname demonstrated that her seat at the table had been handed to her, and she hadn't earned her place there. But she believed in this project and kept her fingers crossed that it would be as successful as she hoped.

The consultants exited the room, and after calling her driver, Nina made her way downstairs. Philippe stopped in front of the building, and she climbed into the back of the black Mercedes with tinted windows.

"Going straight home?" Philippe asked, looking at her in the rearview mirror before returning his eyes to the road.

He was from Guadeloupe, with caramel-colored skin and kind eyes. When Nina's father passed, he had become very protective of her. During the three years she'd been overseas, Nina kept Philippe up to date on her travels, and when she returned to the States last week, she hired him away from the family he'd been working for in the interim.

"Yes."

"Have you eaten?" Philippe asked in his accented English.

"Philippe, you're not my father. I'll get something to eat at home," Nina said, softening the words with a smile.

"Okay. Don't mind me." He laughed, keeping his eyes on the road.

Nina watched the buildings go by. She hadn't talked to Reese since her arrival, and surprisingly, he hadn't called. At some point, they needed to talk, but at least for now he let her set the pace.

Less than an hour later, she relaxed in her apartment, barefoot in shorts and a T-shirt, her thick hair scooped up into a huge, bouncy Afro puff on top of her head as she wound down with a glass of wine and watched the news. Room service should arrive soon with her lobster ravioli.

The phone chirped beside her on the sofa, and she answered when she saw Andy's name.

"Hi, my love," he said, his preferred greeting for her.

"Hi! Are you back?" He should have been back from his trip by Wednesday, but his father had asked him to stick around and help with some projects.

"I have bad news," he said.

"Oh no, what's wrong?"

Andy let out a frustrated sigh. "My father wants me to stay through the weekend and attend a networking thing with some investors. It's full speed ahead on his plans to expand into resorts, the way my mother wanted before she passed."

His voice dropped a little at the end. He still had a hard time talking about his mother, who'd passed away while they were both overseas. She'd flown back with him six months ago to attend the funeral.

"I hate to disappoint you, but I won't be back until *next* week."

"I am disappointed, but I understand. Your father wants you to learn as much as you can, and you've been gone for a while, so it takes time to catch up."

"I knew you'd understand. Hey! Why don't you fly up this weekend and come to the networking event with me, let me show you off."

As disappointed as she was, she did not want to go to New York to network with investors. "Can I take a rain check?"

"Sure. We'll just be working anyway."

She couldn't tell if he was upset but hoped he wasn't. "When exactly will you be back?" she asked.

"Sunday for sure."

"I guess I'll see you then."

"I'll call you tomorrow. Love you."

"Love you, too."

Nina hung up the phone and tried not to dwell on her disappointment. She'd been spoiled while they were overseas and had to get used to him splitting his time between her and his obligations. Andy had been lucky and grateful that his father let him go back on the road after his mother's passing, but now he had to take on the tasks left mainly unattended by her death.

At the sound of gentle knocking, Nina jumped up and skipped down the four steps at the front. Thinking her food had arrived, she swung open the door.

Her heart made an involuntary stutter at the sight of Reese leaning his shoulder in the doorway.

"Reese." She breathed his name in surprise. Her voice came out huskier than it should, and she quickly followed up the greeting by clearing her throat.

His eyes traveled over her in an inappropriately slow review that spent way too much time on her breasts before dropping to the dip in her waist and her bare legs in the skimpy shorts.

"Hi," Reese said, letting male appreciation drip from the two letters.

Heat crawled up Nina's neck. "I, uh, I thought you were room service."

"I could tell you were expecting someone else. Can I come in?"

She hesitated for a second, unsure if allowing him inside her apartment was a good idea. But then she shook off her reservations. She could handle Reese, and the sooner they had their talk, the better.

"Sure." She stepped back, and he strolled in, crowding her at the foot of the stairs as he towered over her. That little space had never seemed so small before, and there was nowhere for her to go except back into the wall.

He pulled a bouquet of flowers from behind his back. "For you." Bright reds, oranges, and yellows burst with contrast against the light blue of his shirt.

Her stomach tightened unexpectedly. She loved flowers— loved to receive them, give them, smell them—particularly ones as lovely as these.

"What's the occasion?" she asked.

19

"Just because," he replied.

Nina took them. "Thank you," she said, doing an excellent job of resisting the urge to lift them to her nose. She didn't want him to know how much she appreciated the kind gesture.

"After you." Reese stepped aside and extended his hand so she could precede him.

He followed her up the stairs, and she became very conscious of her butt in his face because he was right behind her. In the living room, she placed the flowers on a side table and watched Reese take a look around the room.

"So, are you settled in?" he asked.

"Pretty much."

"Then why didn't you call? Tomorrow makes a week since you've been back." Before she could answer, he added, "Still running?"

"I'm not running."

"Could've fooled me."

"Well, I'm not. I've been busy. As a matter of fact, I was at the office today trying to decide whether or not I want to take on the responsibility of running my father's company."

His face shifted into a concerned frown. "And?"

Nina shrugged. "I'm not sure yet. One day. Maybe." She waited for a judgmental remark, but none came.

Reese nodded. "I get that. I have a work decision to make myself."

"What about?"

"The chief information officer of SJ Brands is retiring at the end of the year. My mother wants me to take over, but I'm not sure that's what I want to do."

SJ Brands was the multibillion-dollar conglomerate his mother built over several decades that included fashion, makeup, and furniture lines, while SJ Media was her film company that funded documentaries and produced independent films.

"That leaves about six months to decide."

He laughed a little. "Not that much time. She wants a decision within the next couple of months so that if I turn down the offer, they'll have time to find a replacement."

"Makes sense."

They both fell silent.

Nina wrung her hands together but stopped when his gaze locked on the motion.

"Nina, you don't have to be nervous with me. We've known each other forever."

"But we haven't always been friends," she reminded him. There was a period of over a year when she'd cut him off.

"And I regret that. I regret that because of what I said and did, I can't touch you right now. You're standing so far away from me like you're afraid of me. Are you, Nina? Afraid of me?"

"No," she lied.

She kept a safe distance from him because she couldn't think when he touched her, and unfortunately, Reese was the affectionate type. A hugger like his father, very touchy-feely. That was one of the things she loved—*used* to love—about him.

Her favorite place in the world used to be inside one of his hugs—kissing, laughing, cuddling. She'd sought that same comfort on the first anniversary of her father's death.

"I missed you." He spoke in a husky voice, his purposeful stare so heavy she almost collapsed under its weight.

"Reese."

"Let me finish."

"I can't let you finish because I have something to tell you. First of all, we should not have kissed, and I take full responsibility for initiating it."

He angled his head to the side, looking completely unmoved by her statement. "Are you done?"

"I want to repeat what I've already said in the past, which is that it didn't mean anything."

21

Once again, her words didn't seem to affect him in the least. "Are you done now?"

Letting a heavy breath out through her nose, Nina nodded. "Yes."

"I disagree that the kiss should not have happened. I'm not sorry that it did. It made me realize that you still have feelings for me and that maybe we should try again."

"That is absolutely not what the kiss meant," Nina said in a firm voice.

"That kiss told me everything I needed to know."

"It was a mistake."

"Not to me. I want us to start again. You and me, start over."

His words were tempting—oh, so tempting. But not only was he too late, she had no intention of risking her heart to him again.

"That's not possible," Nina said.

"I know it'll take time for you to trust me, but I'm willing to do whatever it takes to show you we belong together."

Nina shook her head vehemently. "We're not getting back together, Reese."

"You're upset, and you think you can't trust me. But if you give me a chance, you'll see that I've changed. I was nineteen. I broke up with you because I wasn't the right man for you then. I was immature and getting into all kinds of stupid shenanigans that didn't matter but seemed important at the time."

"More important than me," Nina said with a trace of bitterness.

His eyes didn't leave hers. "You deserved better. A good man."

She should tell him now. "You're right, and I found him while traveling."

His eyebrows snapped together in surprise. They stared at each other in the ensuing silence.

"What do you mean, you found him?"

"You and I aren't getting back together, because I'm seeing someone, and it's serious."

CHAPTER 4

*H*ad he heard her correctly?

"What do you mean you're seeing someone? You were single when you left. You were supposed to be helping people on your trip, not finding a man!"

She appeared startled by his angry outburst. To his own ears, he sounded ridiculous, but he couldn't compute what the hell she'd just told him. Nothing she said made sense.

"I have a right to date, and I can't help what happened."

"You're serious?"

"Yes."

"Who is this guy?"

"Coincidentally, he's from the Atlanta area. His name is Andy von Trapp. His family—"

"Hold up, Andy von Trapp? His parents run Von Trapp & Morrison, Inc.? That little weasel?" He remembered Andy from their prep school days. They attended the same academy.

Her eyes widened. "Don't call him that."

"He's a slimeball."

"You're out of line. He's my boyfriend."

She looked genuinely upset, but he didn't give a shit. She could do way better than that dude.

"Back in prep school, we called him Saint Andy because he never did anything wrong and always did whatever his parents told him. He's a goddamn goody-two-shoes."

While Reese and his friends were smoking cigarettes in the bathroom and skipping school in new sports cars they were too young to appreciate, Saint Andy stayed out of trouble and at the end of the day obediently climbed into the chauffeur-driven car that took him to and from school.

"So, he behaved himself and acted like a decent human being, but that was a problem for you and your crew." Nina propped her hands on her hips.

When she put it that way, he really sounded terrible, but Andy was one of his least favorite people.

"He ratted us out senior year by telling the headmaster that we did the senior prank."

Reese had hacked into the school's server and uploaded a short porno clip. The five-minute video had interrupted the headmaster's weekly announcements, broadcasted on flat screens in all the classrooms. Their IT specialist had to shut down the entire network to stop the explicit video from playing.

Reese and his two friends had almost gotten suspended, but his mother stepped in and fixed the problem. To this day, he wasn't sure what she did, but he figured she'd thrown money at the problem to make it go away.

"*He's* the one who told on you?" Nina asked.

"Yeah. Your *boyfriend*," Reese said snidely.

Her delicate jaw tightened. "You've convinced me even more that I've made the right decision. He was a good student who grew into a good man."

Reese chuckled and shook his head. "How'd you meet the saint?"

"Stop calling him that."

"Why? He's such a good man."

"Why can't you—"

A knock sounded on the door, and they both swung their heads in that direction.

"That's my dinner."

He watched Nina walk to the door, his gaze tracing the roundness of her ass and the way the T-shirt fit snug around her torso.

He was anxious to touch her, taste her, savor her lips again. But how the hell was he supposed to win her back with Andy von Trapp's cockblocking ass in the way?

The hotel employee brought in the food on a dome-covered tray that he placed on the dining table near the window.

"Thank you." Nina pulled a few bills from her purse and handed them to the young man.

His eyes widened. "Thank you," he said gratefully before hurrying out.

"How did you two meet?" Reese asked again as soon as they were alone again.

Nina let out an exaggerated sigh. "We met on an organic farm in New Zealand. Naturally, I couldn't believe I was halfway around the world and met someone I was familiar with from the States. I didn't *know* him, but I was familiar with his family name. We got along well and learned we had a lot in common—from food preferences to favorite color. It was as if… I don't know, like we were destined to be together."

That hurt. She didn't have to say that.

"What was he doing in New Zealand?"

"The same thing I was. Traveling and kinda finding himself before he had to get more involved with the family business. His mother gave him time to do whatever he wanted before he had to come back and start at Von Trapp & Morrison. So for more than a year, he joined me on my travels."

"You've been involved with him for over a year?" Reese asked, incredulous.

"Yes," Nina replied in a small voice.

"You sure know how to keep a secret."

That explained the sharp drop-off in communication. He sent messages through her sister, Lindsay, but Nina's responses were rare, and their conversations often cut short. He thought she might have still been upset about the kiss, but the reason was much worse than he'd expected. There was another man in the picture.

She had the grace to look shamefaced and stared down at her feet.

"Von Trapp & Morrison will soon start building resorts, won't they?" Reese asked.

"Yes. They're expanding and setting up an office in New York."

"Isn't that nice. Both of you have an interest in the hotel business. Sounds like a match made in heaven."

Nina leveled a stare at him. "Before Andy's mother died, she wanted to expand into resorts and set up an office in New York. He's carrying on her dream."

"His mother died?"

He hadn't heard, but he and Andy didn't run in the same circles now that they were out of school. They'd never run in the same circles when they were *in* school. Reese had been pretty popular as a wide receiver on the football team, and though he hadn't been good enough to play college ball, he'd been a minor celebrity.

Andy had been quieter, but Reese had always gotten the impression that Andy thought Reese and his friends were beneath him. They never spoke much, but Andy's disdain could be felt from across the room whenever they were in the same vicinity. As if the mere fact that he was not in the limelight made him better than Reese and his friends.

"She passed away six months ago. Look, I think you should go. You're not going to get the answers you came here for."

"We've known each other since senior year. You can't just throw away eleven years of knowing each other."

"I'm not throwing away anything. Friendship is on the table, Reese. That's the only thing I can offer you, the same as always."

He didn't want friendship. He wanted her as his woman. He wanted the right to pull that T-shirt over her head and peel those little gray shorts off her hips and reacquaint himself with every inch of her body—so much fuller and riper than when they'd first met as teens. Yet she'd basically told him that even though she was back in the city, he couldn't touch her.

He'd never expected this turn of events, and he needed time to regroup and reassess the situation. "I'll leave you alone with your dinner." He headed to the door.

Nina swung toward him as he passed. "Reese, did you hear me?"

"I heard you."

He slammed the door on his way out.

* * *

REESE SLAMMED the door at his apartment.

He'd slammed Nina's door. Slammed his car door. Now this door.

"*Fuuuuuck!*" he yelled. Frustration ate him alive every time he thought about Nina with Andy.

His housekeeper, Javier, appeared in the foyer. The older man raised an eyebrow at him. "Bad day?"

"Sorry about that. I thought you'd already left," Reese muttered, moving past him.

Usually, Javier went grocery-shopping on Friday mornings and prepared a couple of meals to get Reese through the weekend until he returned on Monday.

"I'm on my way out. Running a little late today, but dinner is finished and warming in the oven. Do you need anything else before I leave?"

Reese paused on the way back to his bedroom. "No. See you next week."

He used to share a house with his brother, but around the same time Stephan moved his now wife, Roselle, into that house, Reese moved here to give them privacy and finally have his own place.

In the center of the living room, a handmade table made of dark wood that his designer had imported from Costa Rica, sat on a brown and cream area rug, and a seven-shelf gray storage unit across from the single gray L-shaped couched was backlit and contained books, photos, and other items of sentimental value. With gray walls and hardwood floors, the room would be dark if not for the glass wall with open curtains that let in plenty of natural light. However, he kept his bedroom—decorated in similar colors—dark with black-out curtains set to open on a timer during the week to gently wake him up with sunlight instead of the jarring sound of an alarm clock.

In the dressing room, he tossed his shirt in the hamper and then went into the bedroom. Sinking on the edge of the king-size bed, he rested his elbows on his knees and stared at the original Jacob Lawrence painting hanging on the wall.

He mulled Nina's reaction to his words and came to the conclusion that he had been too eager. He'd been fully ready to make a full-court press back into her life when she returned, but that was not to be, and all because of Andy.

He had to recalibrate. Slow down. Adjust the rate at which he came at Nina before he scared her off completely.

Some people might call him calculating, but he didn't like acting on emotion. Reason and logic were his preferred bedfellows. Logical. Methodical.

Yes, he'd messed up years ago, but he and Nina belonged

together. He wanted her, and he was going to get her. When they had been a couple, she'd been into him. Really into him, with feelings as deep and as bottomless as the ocean. He knew because she'd said those exact words to him.

They spent the better part of their senior year together and remained a couple during their first two semesters of college. But they attended universities in different cities, and the temptation to hook up with other women was great. While his boys were having the time of their lives with pretty coeds they'd met at parties or elsewhere on campus, he had to be satisfied with phone sex from his girlfriend hundreds of miles away. It was tough, and her conversations about marriage and kids only fueled his unrest.

She was so sure about what she wanted and had her future all planned. While the furthest in the future he'd thought about was jumping in the shower and jerking off until he could see her again. Rather than cheat, the summer before their sophomore year, he told her he wanted to break things off. But that wasn't the worst of it.

The following week, he and a bunch of friends flew to the Hamptons. While there, a girl he barely knew but who had made several passes at him—Kelly Strong—arrived at the beach, too.

If he'd known what was to come, he wouldn't have done what he did when Kelly showed up at his door. To this day, his biggest regret was opening that damn door.

She was gorgeous and sexy and looked him up and down with a seductive smile. "Hi, Reese."

"What are you doing here?"

She shrugged. "Just being neighborly. Mind if I come in?"

Horny from a night of flirting back and forth at the fire on the beach, that was all it took for him to widen the door and let her in. He was back to doing as he pleased, being a playboy.

Two days later, he returned to Atlanta, and Nina showed up

unexpectedly when he had a few friends over for a party while his mother was out of town. The minute he saw her, he recognized the grave mistake he'd made. He let his hormones make a decision that solely belonged to his heart and head. He realized he had a great relationship, someone who cared about him, checked up on him, and, in general, looked out for him. He decided they could work through the distance.

Then Kelly showed up, and the bomb dropped. Kelly and Nina were enemies, and within one hour of Kelly's arrival, she told Nina *everything*, and apparently in vivid detail.

Nina confronted him in his bedroom, and that's when his sentence without her began. The begging, the pleading, the fight that ensued had torn him apart from the inside out. He'd done everything to hold onto her, including deny that anything happened with Kelly and finally ended by forcing himself on top of Nina on the bed so she couldn't get away.

"Get off of me!" Nina screamed.

"No!"

Reese buried his face in her neck. She refused to touch him in any way, laying her hands flat on the bed, as if he was tainted.

"Get off me, Reese, please. Leave me alone," Nina said, her voice thickened by tears.

"Not until you forgive me. I didn't know."

"Never."

"I messed up. She doesn't mean anything to me."

"I don't mean anything to you. It's only been one damn week."

"You're my everything." He whispered the words into her neck.

"I don't believe you." Tears streamed down the sides of her face and pooled on his temple.

They stayed that way for an eternity until he realized that not only was his temple wet but so was her neck. Not from her tears. But from his.

He sniffed and lifted his head to look down into her eyes. "I'm sorry, Nina."

She kept her gaze on the ceiling. "Get up."

He rolled off her into a sitting position and dragged a palm down his face to erase the evidence of his weakness. He reached for her with the other hand, but she jerked away.

"You will never touch me again." She left him on the bed and fled the house.

She refused to see him or talk to him, and it took more than a year to maneuver his way back into her life. He'd hated himself every single day back then. Hated himself for hurting her and destroying the realest, purest relationship he had.

Over the years, he watched from the sidelines as other men took his place in her life. That was its own special kind of torment. But being without her would have been worse.

When she kissed him on the anniversary of her father's passing, opportunity struck with the speed and heat of lightning. The door cracked open. He'd fully intended to kick it all the way in, but not long after, Nina left the country.

At this point, he should leave well enough alone and accept that he really and truly missed his chance. After all, she just told him she was involved with another man—in a *serious* relationship. But he couldn't get that kiss off his mind. He couldn't accept that it was a fluke, ensconced in the past, never to be repeated. He couldn't accept that all that was left between them was mere friendship. Not when he sensed she still had feelings for him.

Nah, friendship was wholly and unequivocally off the table.

He lost Nina by his own actions and intended to win her back the same way. No way could he leave her alone.

He wouldn't be Reese Brooks if he did.

CHAPTER 5

*S*he was a vision in the satin bridesmaid's dress. There were two other bridesmaids, but Nina outshined them both. Her chestnut skin brightened the champagne color, instead of the other way around. The plunging neckline and spaghetti straps presented her breasts as a feast for the eyes. Reese licked his lips. He'd hardly looked at anyone else since he escorted her down the aisle.

Andy hadn't attended Lindsay and Malik's wedding, and he wasn't at the reception, either. Good. Reese didn't know how he'd react when he saw him, and at least today he'd have unrestricted time with Nina. At the moment, he hung back and let people who didn't know she was back in the country or hadn't seen her before today spend time with her.

He ambled over to where his cousin Ivy and older sister Ella were standing and whispering. Ivy's husband, Lucas, was on the other side of the ballroom. Lucas had developed a close relationship with Lindsay, mentoring her and introducing her to his literary agent. She gave him much of the credit for her success.

Ivy smiled as Reese approached. Tall and statuesque, she was his deceased uncle's only daughter. She worked with her four brothers at Johnson Enterprises in Seattle and oversaw the restaurant part of the business, Ivy's, a fine-dining restaurant, and The Brew Pub, a casual dining establishment.

Reese slipped between both women and gave her a hug. This was the first time he'd had a chance to speak to her today.

"Did you bring the kids?" he asked.

She had a daughter in middle school and a toddler son.

"No, we left them at home. We're flying back tomorrow. How have you been?"

"Hanging in there."

"Aunt Sylvie said you're taking over the CIO position next year?"

Reese groaned.

Ella laughed. "Mother wants him to and keeps dropping major hints."

Ella was second-in-command, the vice president of operations overseeing all of their mother's companies under SJ Brands and SJ Media. Like their mother, her skin was much darker than his, and she'd inherited Sylvie's light-brown eyes. Her long hair was pulled into an intricate twist at her nape, and she wore a burgundy wrap dress with black high heels.

Polished and professional, she'd come a long way since marrying a guy who'd chipped away at her confidence. The whole family was relieved when they finally divorced. Her new husband, a former Atlanta police detective, was a much better fit.

"So, you don't want the job?" Ivy asked.

"I do, except it would mean less time doing the hands-on work I enjoy, and more time in meetings and dealing with paperwork, contracts, and going to conferences."

For now, he savored the moments when he could lose himself in work—work he'd enjoyed since childhood. Computers and technology had been his first love, long before Nina captured his heart. Rebuilding computers and troubleshooting error messages had helped him navigate the tumultuous emotions he experienced watching his parents fight and ultimately divorce. Their split didn't only tear apart the family, it wreaked havoc on his conscience, creating a mess of confusion around parental loyalty and the sanctity of marriage.

For that reason, he'd decided long ago that he didn't want to get married or have kids. Life was complicated enough without adding the problematic idea of two people joining their lives together until death. And anyway, who said two people couldn't make a life together and be happy without a piece of paper? As far as he was concerned, that was bullshit, cooked up by societal standards that were no longer relevant in modern times.

"In that case, I wish you luck. Aunt Sylvie always gets what she wants, doesn't she?"

Ella nodded and glanced at her brother. "Always. You know she's not going to rest until you say yes."

"I still have time to decide," Reese said.

Lucas came over and extended his hand to his wife. "Do you two mind if I borrow my wife for a dance?" He was a big guy with a beard and Southern accent to match his Georgia roots.

"Not at all," Ella said.

"Go right ahead," Reese said.

Ivy gave them a little wave and slipped away with her husband to the dance floor.

"Did you already get Mother a gift for her birthday tomorrow?" Ella asked.

"Shit, I forgot."

Two occasions one never forgot for Sylvie Johnson—Mother's Day and her birthday.

"Tsk, tsk. Why can't you and Stephan ever remember her birthday? It's the same date every year."

He and his brother had had near-misses over the years, but Ella always pulled them through.

"Because we suck."

"True. Lucky for you, I've saved the day again. A few months ago, the House of Robar designed limited-edition chocolate diamond rings, and Mother didn't get one. She was livid."

"Doesn't she have enough diamonds?"

"One can never have enough diamonds, darling," Ella said, mimicking their mother's lofty tone.

Reese laughed. "One day she's going to catch you doing that."

Ella grinned. "I hope not. She'll probably disown me. Anyway, I was able to get one, and *you* scheduled it to be delivered to the penthouse tomorrow before she goes to dinner with Father. You can pay me back later."

Reese released a sigh of relief. "Thanks, Ella. You're a lifesaver."

"I know."

He could tell she wanted to say more. "What?"

Her gaze traveled to where Nina sat at a table, chatting with a mutual male friend. She let out a laugh that brightened her features, and his gut twisted.

"Are you still going to try to win Nina back?"

His siblings knew all about his relationship with Nina, the kiss, and the hope that sprang in his chest because of it.

"I guess you didn't hear." Reese shoved his right hand in his pants pocket and rolled his shoulders. Just thinking about her with another man made him tense. He couldn't stand the thought of Andy putting his hands all over her. Loving on her.

"Hear what?"

"She came back with a boyfriend."

Ella's eyes widened. "A what? Are you sure?"

"Yeah, I'm sure. She told me. Andy von Trapp. They met overseas."

"Oh, Reese, I'm so sorry. I wish—"

"I'm good. Don't even worry about it."

Ella's eyes narrowed, which he pretended not to notice. "What are you up to?"

"What makes you think I'm up to something?"

"Because I know you."

"The only thing I'm up to is winning back the woman I love."

"You just said she has a man."

"A temporary setback. I have to plan a little differently, that's all."

"Oh, boy. Reese, I know how much you love Nina, but she has a right to move on, even after the kiss."

"Don't preach to me, Ella. I know what I'm doing."

"Do you?" she hissed.

"Yes," Reese said in a tight voice. "You want me to give up, but I can't do that."

It didn't matter that for the past three years she'd barely kept in touch. It didn't matter that he often had to be the one to reach out because he wanted her never to doubt that he cared. She'd returned with a boyfriend, but no way was he giving up. He'd been patient long enough—too long. That was the problem.

Andy von Trapp merely represented a bump in the road, one he could easily drive right over.

"Reese—"

"I've made up my mind. Nina's the one for me, and nothing is going to change that. I've been patient, I've given her space, but all of that changes now that she's back for good. I'm making my move, and I don't give a fuck about Andy or any man who *thinks* he can stand in my way."

Neither of them said a word for a while. Ella stared down at the floor as if asking it to give her the right words to change his mind.

Finally, she raised her head and spoke quietly. "I kinda always figured you two would get back together, but after ten years…"

"Mother and Father reconciled after fifteen."

"But they love each other," Ella said, her voice going even quieter, in a gentler tone.

Pain forked through him, but he straightened and held his head high. "She still has feelings for me. I know she does. I can feel it."

"She has a man."

"Your point?"

"Someone's going to get hurt, and I don't want it to be you."

"It won't."

Ella pursed her lips. "One more point, and then I'm done. But, maybe Nina's not the one for you, and there's someone else out there who is—your perfect fit. You've been so focused on her, I don't think you've given anyone else a chance. Maybe you should."

Not once had the thought crossed his mind. "You done?" Reese asked tonelessly.

Ella threw up her hands. "All right. I won't bother you about this anymore. Don't forget to call Mother tomorrow."

"I won't."

She squeezed his arm and walked away.

Now was a good time to strike up a conversation with Nina. Reese went to the open bar and ordered an IPA beer for himself and a chocolate martini for Nina.

Then he headed in her direction.

CHAPTER 6

Only a few couples were on the dance floor, and one of them was Malik and Lindsay. The band was in the middle of a sultry slow jam, courtesy of a lovely Black woman wearing hoop earrings with a husky voice that deserved to be heard by millions instead of slightly more than a hundred guests in a hotel ballroom.

Nina saw Reese crossing the floor with purposeful strides in her direction. She didn't want a scene at her sister's reception and hoped he didn't plan to start an argument about her relationship with Andy. When he left the other day, she had the distinct impression that he had not given up.

He stopped beside the table.

"Hey, Dee, mind if I grab my girl for a few minutes?" He kept his eyes on her, and she kept her eyes on him.

"Nah, man, I don't mind. I'll talk to you later, Nina. It was good seeing you."

"Good seeing you, too."

Their mutual male acquaintance stood and walked away, and Reese set a martini in front of Nina. "For you."

First flowers, now a chocolate martini. She arched an inquisitive brow but accepted it. "Thank you."

He sat down in the vacated seat beside her, fine when Dee sat there but now seemed too close. "You're welcome. I know it's your favorite."

Of course he did, because they knew everything about each other since they had remained friends through the years. She knew that his preferred drinks were a strong brandy or a crisp IPA like the one in his glass. The night at her apartment, when he held her sobbing against his chest, she had tasted the bitter beer in his mouth when they kissed.

At the oddest of times, she still tasted that flavor and couldn't bring herself to drink one because it reminded her so much of how *he* had tasted that night and the scent on his breath—that she became, to her alarm…aroused.

Eying Reese as he took a sip of beer, Nina ran her tongue along the inside of her mouth, reliving the flavor with phantom remnants that remained on her taste buds. Reese set the glass on the table, and when he moved, the muscles under his white shirt rippled and pushed against the fabric. He sat back, at ease in the chair with his legs spread and his left hand resting on his upper thigh in a casual but masculine pose.

Did his mouth already smell and taste like the beer?

"Where's your boyfriend?"

Nina crossed her legs. "He couldn't make it. He's in New York."

"Too bad," Reese said, without a smidgen of sincerity in his voice. "Having a good time, though?"

"Yes. You?" Nina shifted, wondering where the conversation was going, considering the last time they talked.

"Nah. Not really." His answer surprised her.

"Why not?"

"Because I made a mistake, and I've been trying to figure out how to apologize."

"What would you be apologizing for?"

"For acting like an ass."

"Which day was that?" She allowed a small, teasing smile to come to her lips.

He laughed softly. "Oh, it's like that? I'm such a regular asshole you need me to narrow down the day?"

Nina sipped her martini.

Reese bit his lip, eyeing her with amusement in his eyes. "All right, we'll play it your way. I'm sorry for acting like a jerk when you told me you had a boyfriend. Your announcement took me by surprise."

She nodded, her face becoming somber. "For the record, that's not the way I wanted you to find out—blurting it out like that."

"I kind of forced your hand."

"I don't want things to be awkward between us, Reese."

"I don't, either. That's why I had to apologize and let you know that I acknowledge your relationship with Andy."

"Acknowledge it? What does that mean?"

"You told me that you're in a relationship with Andy, and I accept that's the truth."

He sounded perfectly reasonable, but that was an odd way to talk about her relationship. She took a good look at him, searching for signs of trickery.

"I want you to be happy," he said in a grave voice.

The words hit hard, and she took a minute to regain balance, then swallowed a lump in her throat. "Thank you. I want the same for you."

"Maybe one day," he said, looking intently at her.

"You have a lot of women friends, but you're not happy?" Nina asked.

As a senior in high school, Reese already had a reputation as a ladies' man, due to his popularity as an athlete. He was the richest and most entitled student at a school filled with rich and entitled students. She fell for him anyway, a young man the exact opposite of everything she wanted in a boyfriend. Not much had changed over the years.

He still had a big appetite for women. They knew so many of the same people, the whispers and gossip made their way to her ears, whether she wanted to know about his escapades or not. A few women lasted for a while, but most cycled in and out of his life with surprising frequency.

"How should I answer that question?" he asked.

"Honestly." Nina held her breath as she awaited his response.

"Okay." Resting his right ankle on his knee, Reese leaned toward her. He looked directly into her eyes, and for a moment, they were the only people in the room. Two wounded souls trying to make peace. "What I'm about to say doesn't sound nice, but it's the truth. None of those women mean anything to me. I know what I want, and if I could turn back time—"

"Don't." Nina turned away from him, clenching her fingers in her lap. She always cut him off whenever she sensed he was about to say something about his feelings for her.

She watched his brother, Stephan, pull his wife, Roselle, onto the dance floor and let silence descend between them. Meanwhile, the background noise of the balladeer crooning into the microphone, and guests laughing and talking, remained constant.

Reese shifted back and straightened in the chair. "Have you talked to my mother today?"

Nina appreciated the abrupt change in topic and breathed easier. "Yes. She chastised me for not coming to see her and invited me to brunch next week. I felt awful, but I've been preoccupied at Winthrop headquarters, trying to catch up with everyone, and then there's a project I've been working on—the volunteer program I want to roll out company-wide." She took a deep breath. "Anyway, I'm going to see her next week."

"That will make her happy."

"I should have made time right away."

"She's not going to love you any less."

Sylvie liked Nina, and Nina liked her. Their mutual admiration didn't waver after she and Reese broke up.

"She doesn't love me."

"Yes, she does. She wanted you as a daughter-in-law." He took a sip of beer.

Nina's eyes opened wide. "What?"

"You didn't know that? She still does and was disappointed when we broke up."

"We were teenagers."

"Doesn't matter. You were her idea of the perfect daughter-in-law. After we broke up, she gave me the cold shoulder for a few weeks."

Her mouth fell open. "Stop."

"I swear. Ask Simone or Ella if you don't believe me. I'm still not sure she's forgiven me for screwing that up."

"You're exaggerating."

"Ask her when you see her next week."

"I'm not asking your mother that." She side-eyed him.

Reese laughed, and Nina relaxed a little more. She could do this. She could be friends with him. They could go back to normal. They had to.

"I have an idea. How about I meet you over at my parents' place, then you and I can get some ice cream and hit Centennial Park like we could have done if you'd let me know about your few trips back."

She had returned to the States a handful of times over the past three years but never notified Reese. "How did you know I've been back?"

"Come on, you really think I didn't know the times you came back?"

She should have known. They had mutual friends, and Stephan and Lindsay were close.

43

"I know you came back and didn't see me, didn't call."

Nina shifted guiltily. "They were short visits. I didn't have time."

"You could have made time. You could have called, but we're not going to dwell on that. I'll meet you at my parents' house next week. But tonight, you owe me a dance." He pushed back his chair and stood.

"Owe?"

"Yes. Since you never called when you visited over the years."

"You don't like to dance."

Reese extended his hand. "I'm making an exception today. Don't leave me hanging in front of all these people."

"That's blackmail."

She placed her hand in his and instant electricity coursed through her palm. Heat flamed her chest, and on shaky legs, she followed behind Reese and noticed the eyes that tracked their movement to the dance floor, as if everyone who knew about their past watched to see the outcome of a simple dance.

She allowed him to pull her close, but when he rested his hands on her waist, she tensed.

"Relax. Put your arms around me," Reese whispered. His mouth to her cheek was a ghost of a touch. She barely felt it, but her body throbbed with the scent of hops on his breath and the prospect of his lips on hers.

Her belly trembled as he squeezed her closer, turning them in a slow circle and smoothing his hands up and down her spine. They were standing too close—torso to torso, pelvis to pelvis, thigh to thigh.

Nina released a chest-stretching sigh of frustration and longing. How could he still do this to her after all this time? How could he still make her *feel* so much when she needed to have nerves of steel and wanted to be indifferent to the memories he reactivated in her mind. Memories that reminded her he wasn't all bad.

He could be thoughtful and funny, and as a couple, he always did what other boys didn't. Very affectionate, he held her hand and kissed her in public. If they were chilling on the sofa, he'd pull her legs across his as they watched TV, or their shoulders had to touch as they ate dinner beside each other in a booth. She didn't always remember to reach for him, but he always remembered to reach for her—walking down the sidewalk, at the movies, or giving her fingers a squeeze of encouragement.

Suddenly, Nina became aware that people were leaving the dance floor. She'd been so lost in memories that she didn't notice the music had stopped. She eased away, and Reese let her go.

His jaw hardened, and emotion shadowed his dark brown eyes. "Thanks for the dance," he said huskily.

Nina nodded. "Sure."

She backed away and then hurried from the dance floor, tossing a weak but reassuring smile at her sister, whose worried eyes followed her across the carpet.

Nina rushed into the bathroom and shut herself in one of the stalls. She leaned back against the door and listened as a woman one stall over hummed a tune, but she didn't recognize the song. She couldn't concentrate on anything else because thoughts of Reese filled her head.

Her nipples were tight, and the flesh between her thighs twitched and ached. Closing her eyes, she took two deep breaths. She felt guilty as if she'd done something wrong.

She'd always thought of cheating as the sexual joining of two bodies, but could dirty thoughts be considered cheating? If she wanted a man who wasn't her boyfriend, if she were wet simply from touching him, did *that* count as cheating, too?

CHAPTER 7

"Welcome, my darling!" Sylvie Johnson squeezed both of Nina's hands between hers as she entered the penthouse.

Nina had run into Reese in the lobby, so he was right behind her.

"Thank you," Nina said.

She always felt a little intimidated in the presence of Reese's mother. Sylvie, elegant and beautiful, had a big personality. Nina admired her, but at the same time, didn't know quite how to take her.

She came from a very wealthy family, but she'd opted not to go into the family business and had built her own empire. Nina longed to be as knowledgeable in business as Sylvie. Unfortunately, she didn't have the know-how, and her lack of confidence inhibited her from doing better.

"You look lovely. Doesn't she look lovely, Reese?"

Nina blushed. There was nothing special about the way she'd dressed. She'd purposely kept her outfit simple—jeans and a polka-dot blouse with a high neckline—so as not to draw Reese's attention. She still felt guilty about what happened at the wedding reception, but she believed much of the problem stemmed from being away from Andy. With him back in town, she expected her attraction to Reese to diminish.

"Yes, she does look lovely," Reese said.

"And how are you, darling?" Sylvie asked.

"Fine." Reese gave his mother a quick kiss on the cheek.

"I'm wearing the diamond ring you bought for my birthday. I love it so much. Thank you."

"You're welcome, Mother."

Sylvie displayed her fingers to show off a ring with a chocolate diamond to Nina.

"It's gorgeous," Nina gushed.

"Yes, it is. However did you know I wanted this? I don't believe I ever mentioned it to you," Sylvie said to Reese.

"You must have, and although I'm not perfect, I do pay attention."

"That you do." Her gaze rested on Nina again. "Some of my friends complain about their sons and their indifference toward dates of importance, but I have no such complaints. I'm lucky to have two wonderful boys who always remember my birthday and manage to get exactly what I want, every single time, even when I don't remember discussing those gift choices with them. It's as if someone else has told them what I wanted." Sylvie laughed daintily. "Oscar is in the sitting room. Follow me. We can't wait to hear all about your adventures."

Stunned, it took several seconds for Nina to follow.

Does she know, she mouthed to Reese.

I don't know, he mouthed with a worried expression.

Nina stifled a chuckle with her hand.

Wearing tan slacks and a cream blouse with billowy sleeves, Sylvie led them to the sitting room where her husband sat in an armchair, reading a magazine. As soon as he saw them, he stood.

"Nina, it's good to see you." Oscar Brooks was a handsome older man with graying hair and light-colored skin and dark eyes in direct contrast to his wife's dark brown skin and light brown eyes.

His genuine smile warmed her insides as she melted into one of his bear hugs.

"It's good to see you, too, Mr. Brooks." Nina sat on the sofa beside Sylvie.

The older woman brushed her long hair over one shoulder and crossed her legs. Reese sat in the other armchair.

"Reese told me you and Andy von Trapp are a couple? Is that correct?"

Get right to business. That didn't take long. Nina glanced quickly at Reese, whose face remained impassive.

"Yes."

"And you knew him before you left the country?"

"Actually, no. I'd heard of him and his family but didn't know them personally, which makes how we met kind of funny. I was doing volunteer work on an organic farm in New Zealand when we ran into each other—if you can believe that."

"You don't say. That's quite a coincidence."

Was she being sarcastic?

"You probably know his family. They're in the process of opening a New York office. Now that he's joined the family business, Andy will be shuttling back and forth between here and there on a regular basis." At least, that's what he'd told her, all of which had come as a surprise.

"That's right. After Andy's parents divorced, they decided to stay in business together, if I recall," Sylvie said.

"Yes, that's correct."

"It was so sad when I heard his mother died. From complications of the flu, of all things." Sylvie tutted. "Andy's mother was the real brains of the operation, a shark when it comes to real estate. It's such a shame that for years she didn't work outside of the home, at her husband's insistence. All of that changed when they divorced, of course, and the business started doing much better. Who knows how that business could have flourished if she had been in charge from the beginning? As I understand it, they're going into resorts now."

"That's correct. Before she passed, Andy's mother planned to take the company in that direction."

"I see. Tell me, do *you* plan to work if you and Andy get married?"

"Mother!"

Oscar let out a heavy sigh.

Sylvie looked from one to the other with fake innocence. "I simply asked a question. You don't mind, do you, Nina?"

"Um...no."

Nina took a deep breath and prepared to let Reese's parents know, the same as she'd informed Reese, that her relationship with Andy was solid. If Oscar and Sylvie held onto any idea that she and Reese were getting back together, they needed to rid themselves of that notion right now.

"If Andy and I decide to get married, we'll work out those issues beforehand. He's a great guy, very understanding. I'm certain I've found my soul mate."

The room went quiet.

A cool mask slipped over Sylvie's features. "Is that right?" she asked in a low voice.

Nina nodded and scanned the room. Oscar glanced at Reese, whose jaw had tightened so hard, he might very well grind his molars to dust.

"Well, that's a shame, isn't it, Reese?" Sylvie tossed a glance in her son's direction.

"Not if she's happy," Reese said with a tight smile.

"Tell us about your trip," Oscar interjected, sending a hard look at his wife, which she purposely ignored by dusting nonexistent lint off her pants leg.

49

Before Nina could answer, the house manager, Trevor, entered the room.

"Brunch is ready," he announced.

Relieved at the interruption, Nina stood first. They all went into the dining room, where Trevor had prepared a spread that was way too much for four people, with all the food set on elegant white serving dishes—family-style—in the center of the table.

Prosciutto-wrapped pineapple spears shared the table with individual fruit cups. Another plate held buttery croissants, and yet another contained a loaf of Trevor's delicious gingerbread coffee cake, four hefty slices already cut into it, which Nina had smelled as soon as she hit the doorway. Creamy egg salad had been scooped onto baguette slices and sprinkled with chives. As if that wasn't enough, as they settled into their chairs and Nina took a sip of her Bellini, Trevor reappeared with a steaming bowl of freshly made shrimp and grits.

"Bon appétit," Oscar said, raising his glass.

Nina spent much of the next couple of hours fielding questions from Oscar and Sylvie. She caught them up on her work overseas, the people she met and served in each country, the food she ate, and the two times she'd fallen so ill she'd almost abandoned her plans and returned home for good.

She told them about the hours she spent snorkeling and fishing off the coast of Belize and then grilled the catches of the day with her newfound friends. Despite all the fresh food she ate, she occasionally missed eating a fried chicken plate at her favorite downtown restaurant and missed good ol' American pizza from Notte, one of her favorite Italian restaurants in the city.

The entire time she talked, she could feel Reese watching her, and each time she glanced at him, he was. For the most part, she kept Andy out of the recounting of her stories and relaxed into the familiarity of people she knew and their welcoming conversation. By the end of the visit, she felt rejuvenated, but a twinge of regret nicked her chest that her relationship with this family was not as close as it used to be.

Finally, she and Reese said their goodbyes and took the elevator toward the first floor.

"That was fun, although the first part of the visit was a little uncomfortable. Your mother wasn't as subtle as she usually is."

"When has my mother ever been subtle?"

"True. But she took me by surprise with a few of her comments."

"All of my siblings are married, and I'll be thirty soon. The pressure is on." He kept his eyes on the doors in front of him.

She wanted to respond but held her tongue. Sylvie was wasting her time because Reese had made no secret of the fact that he didn't want children and didn't want to get married. He'd made that decision a long time ago when he witnessed his parents' acrimonious divorce.

She glanced sideways at him but couldn't figure out what he was thinking. "Are we still going for ice cream?" she asked, in an effort to not only make conversation but leave behind more incendiary topics.

They stepped into the foyer of the building.

"Absolutely. I know how much you love ice cream." As if he realized his lukewarm attitude toward her gave off a bad vibe, Reese smiled suddenly.

And when he did, *her* attitude changed. His grin charmed a smile from her lips and eased what little tension existed between them.

Not for the first time, she noted the angles of his face, as if he'd been put together with meticulous care. He was a handsome man, so it was no surprise women flocked to him. Why did she ever think she could keep the attention of a man like this?

"You know me too well," she said in a low voice, emotional all of a sudden.

The valet pulled up, and Nina stared at the amber-colored Mercedes SUV in disbelief.

"Is this yours? How did you get one?" she demanded.

She'd been on the waiting list for months now, desperate to get one of the limited-edition vehicles when she returned to the States. Each one could be customized to its owner's specifications. Despite being wealthy, she didn't usually care about luxuries and could be comfortable almost anywhere. But she was loyal to Mercedes, and when she learned about this special-edition vehicle, she'd wanted one.

"Yes, it's mine," Reese said smugly.

"Billionaires suck."

Technically, Reese wasn't a billionaire, as he hadn't received the proceeds from his trust fund yet. On January first, after he turned thirty, he'd receive over a billion dollars in money and assets. He was also an heir to his mother's multibillion-dollar company, which would make him even richer one day.

Reese laughed. "Don't hate." He opened the passenger door to let her in.

"Can I drive?" Nina asked.

"*Hell* no."

"Why not?"

"Because you drive like shit. It's your sole flaw. I'm not risking my new car with you behind the wheel. Come on, let's go." He snapped his fingers for her to hurry up.

"I thought when you criticized my driving you were just kidding." He'd always told her she was an awful driver and refused to ride with her.

"I was dead serious."

"I'm a great driver," Nina said, standing a little taller.

"You're a terrible driver. You drive too fast, and you have a nasty attitude when you're behind the wheel. We both know that's why you have a chauffeur. No, you can't drive my car."

"I can't believe this."

"Believe it."

"You get on my nerves."

"Yeah, yeah. Get in."

Nina climbed in and sat in the car with her arms crossed. She jealously inhaled the new car smell and eyed the sumptuous leather, wood-grain interior, and touch-screen dashboard that controlled everything from the radio to the diagnostics to the Wi-Fi.

When Reese climbed in, he glanced at her, and the right corner of his mouth lifted into a sexy half-smile. "Buckle up and stop pouting."

She did as he asked but cut her eyes at him, and he laughed.

His laughter was so rich and smooth. So pure and real. As he drove into the street, she experienced an unexpected pull of attraction, a sensation she hadn't experienced in a long time. A longing, an aching, to just…touch him, to smooth her palm over his short hair or brush her lips to his jaw.

Her breath caught, and she quickly turned away to stare out the window.

That was…unexpected and dangerous. The slight burn in her chest was not new. It had prompted her to kiss him three and a half years ago.

It was familiar. A warning.

A warning that spending time with Reese Brooks was not a good idea.

CHAPTER 8

*H*eat hovered over the city, promising a hotter-than-usual summer. Ice cream was an excellent way to cool off in the high temperatures.

Nina ordered two scoops in a cup—dulce de leche and chunky chocolate chip.

"I'll take strawberry and chocolate," Reese said from beside her.

"You're allergic to strawberries. Do not give him strawberry ice cream," she said to the woman behind the counter.

"You always do this. It's not like I'll die. I only break out in hives."

She waved her hand in his direction as if to say, *See?* to the clerk.

The woman smiled at Reese. "Since you can't have strawberry, what other flavors would you like with the chocolate? You can sample any of the others."

"I want chocolate and strawberry," he said.

"*Reese,*" Nina said, turning his name into two syllables.

"I don't have a lot of choices," he said.

Nina placed a hand on her hip. "There are literally dozens of choices here, but you're so picky you refuse to eat anything other than vanilla, chocolate, or strawberry."

"I don't need rocks, sticks, and stones in my ice cream."

Nina rolled her eyes and faced the clerk. "Give him vanilla and chocolate, please."

"I want chocolate and strawberry," Reese told the woman, dead serious.

"Do not give him strawberry ice cream."

Unsure what to do, the clerk smiled uneasily and glanced at the other customers, as if they could rescue her.

Reese sighed. "Since she's the boss of me, give me vanilla and chocolate."

"Thank you," Nina said with a self-satisfied smirk. She scooped a spoonful of dulce de leche in her mouth. The sweet caramel flavor almost made her moan out loud.

"Good?" Reese asked.

"Mmm-hmm." She dug in for another scoop. "It's sooo g—"

He wasn't looking at the ice cream. He was looking at her. Or, more specifically, her mouth. Self-consciously, she wiped her tongue over her cool lips.

"Looks good," he said in a low voice.

Her chest tightened, and she refocused on the dessert, dipping the spoon into one scoop and then the other.

"Here you go." The clerk handed Reese his order and then rang up the total for both.

He paid, and they left the shop in silence.

On the short walk to Centennial Olympic Park, Reese did most of the talking by catching her up on recent happenings among mutual acquaintances. Nina took that time to reset. Back at the parlor, he'd looked at her in the same way that he'd done in the past. She'd rarely caught a glimpse of that expression in his eyes but knew how to describe it.

Hunger. Nothing but pure, unadulterated hunger. Not for the creamy dessert in her cup. For *her*.

They arrived at Centennial Olympic Park, a legacy of the 1996 Olympic Games. Twenty-two acres located near other tourist attractions such as the Georgia Aquarium, the World of Coca-Cola, the Center for Civil Rights and Human Rights, and the College Football Hall of Fame.

They strolled over to the Fountain of Rings and sat on the long row of cement steps where they had a good view of the kids darting through the water shooting up from the ground. With their parents looking on, some tried in vain to avoid getting wet by running between the streams, while others embraced the fun and took the direct hit, laughing and squawking as they got soaked.

Although Nina had enjoyed her travels, she'd missed her hometown, and scenes like this reminded her of the simple pleasures. She spooned more of the blissful treat into her mouth, which cooled her body in the Atlanta heat.

Reese's expression softened as he watched the children playing in the water, which made her wonder why he didn't want any of his own. Was he still utterly opposed to the idea of fatherhood?

She was a daddy's girl, and after her parents split, she'd always wanted to have a family of her own with both parents in the home instead of what she'd experienced—being shuttled back and forth across town to spend time with one parent or the other, according to court documents.

She'd had all these fantasies about her and Reese raising a family together and growing old together, which had been tossed out the window when he told her, frankly but gently, that he didn't want to get married and didn't want kids.

"So, what are your plans for The Winthrop Hotel Group?"

"Honestly?"

"Yes, honestly."

"Remember my volunteerism idea I told you about? It's called The Winthrop Helping Hands Program, and the results after one year of testing came back very positive. Employee morale improved, productivity improved, and customer service scores increased across the board." She explained the details of the program to him and finished by saying, "It's a radical idea, but it worked, and we're going to roll out the program to the entire company."

"That's great, but why don't you look more excited?" He dipped into his ice cream and ate a spoonful of vanilla.

"Because if it's successful, that's wonderful, but once we tweak the program and have someone to oversee it, what will I do? Do I go to work at the company?"

"You could. Why couldn't you?" He looked genuinely perplexed.

"I don't have any hotel management experience. Andy..." Reese stiffened at the mention of her fiancé's name, but if they were going to be friends, he'd have to get used to hearing his name. "Andy thinks I should leave hotel management to the people who do the work day in and day out."

"It's your company."

"But I don't have any experience, and running a multimillion-dollar company takes intelligence and hard work, and knowledge about the field."

"No one is born knowing how to run a business. But you're smart, and you work hard, and you care about people. That will more than make up for your lack of knowledge. You should absolutely be more involved in the running of your company."

"They're doing fine without me." She swirled her spoon through the softened ice cream, blending the two flavors so that chocolate chunks cozied up to caramel swirls.

"Maybe they are doing fine without you, but that doesn't mean they can't do better."

Nina cradled the cup in her hand. "I really do want to do more. I could give it a try," she said hesitantly.

"You should," Reese said in a firm voice. He was so confident in his abilities and knew exactly what he wanted to do. He didn't care about running his mother's company—all he cared about was those darn computers and making sure the network ran like a well-greased machine.

Reese could spend hours working, and she used to love watching him do it. He wouldn't move to eat or get a drink. She hated to disturb him, but her selfish self would go to him anyway, in need of a kiss or a snuggle. His focused face looked so sexy as he sat hunched over the computer, working on code or whatever.

Sometimes he'd be so engrossed he wouldn't hear her enter the room, which meant she'd have a minute or two to watch him undetected before he finally noticed her presence. Then he'd invite her in and spend the next few minutes explaining the current project, and she'd sit on his lap, basking in his attention and the inclusion in his work, comfortable in his embrace and—

Don't do this. Don't reminisce.

"You're focusing on the volunteer aspect of the business because that's where you're comfortable, and you think that's all you can manage, but I don't believe that," Reese said.

"If I step into a leadership role, I have to know what I'm doing. I don't want to fall flat on my face. We have thousands of employees around the globe, and I can't look bad."

"*They* work for *you*. *They* have to impress *you*, not the other way around."

"It's not that simple, Reese, and you know it."

"Do you believe your father was a smart man?"

"Of course. He was brilliant."

"Would a smart man leave his entire fortune to someone who couldn't handle it? If he thought you couldn't, he would have split up the business or found another way to take care of you while making sure someone else is in charge. He left *you* in charge. You own everything. He believed in you. Isn't it time you believe in yourself?"

She'd never thought of it that way.

"You're right. Besides, I have two consultants to help me. I need to put them to work on helping me with a plan to take over the company."

"Good. And you shouldn't let anyone make you feel like you can't handle the work."

Nina stiffened. She regretted mentioning Andy's comment. "It's not a big deal."

Reese angrily scraped the bottom of the paper cup. "You know what Ella went through with her ex. He stifled her. She hid her intelligence and gave up her career for that guy, and we —her family—had to watch from the sidelines as she contorted herself into someone else to make him happy, and he still wasn't happy. And she sure as hell wasn't."

"My relationship with Andy isn't like that," Nina insisted.

"Not now, but it could be."

"I'm not changing for him, but marriage is about compromise."

"What is he compromising about?" Reese demanded.

"I didn't agree to spend time with you so you could badmouth my boyfriend."

"I just asked a question," Reese said.

"Don't ask questions about him because your questions aren't innocent." Fuming, Nina set the cup beside her. The ice cream pooled in the bottom, a thin soupy liquid that no longer looked appetizing. "You have no right to talk about him."

"I can talk about whomever I damn well please. It's my goddamn tongue. He's busy going back and forth to New York although you thought he'd be spending more time with you here—and don't deny it, because I know I'm right. You expect me to believe this is the man for you?" Reese snorted in disgust. "You won't be satisfied with an absentee boyfriend. You like having your man near, spending time with him, going out. Sharing laughs."

"You know me so well," Nina said sarcastically.

Nina didn't know what else to say because Reese had accurately summed up her desires in a partner.

Her eyes followed the children running through the water. Some of the parents paid attention. Some snapped photos. Some talked on the phone and didn't pay attention nearly as closely as they should. But they were all parents, and she wanted that life. She wanted the husband and the children. She wanted to come home to someone. She wanted to cuddle with her husband after the kids were tucked into bed. She wanted stability, normalcy, love. Sometimes you had to sacrifice to get what you want.

Looking off into the distance, she finally found the words. "You know what my mom told me after you and I broke up? She said I needed to find a happy place, like she did after my dad left her. One place where I can go to recharge. Regroup. A place that brings me peace...and happiness. It could be a favorite resort or simply a favorite restaurant where the food is good, and though you sit in the corner, everybody knows your name and makes you feel welcomed. My mother loves our Newport cottage on the beach. If she could go there all the time, she would.

"I never took her advice back then. I wallowed in self-pity and, eventually, I didn't hurt anymore." She swallowed. "When my dad died, I felt lost for a long time, and then I remembered what my mother said. 'Find your happy place.' I still haven't found it, but I found something close. I loved traveling, and I loved the work I did helping people. That's how I met Andy, and we share the same beliefs and want the same things out of life.

"So maybe our ideas don't always line up perfectly, but I won't let you badmouth him." She finally became brave enough to look at Reese. Like his mother, he hid his emotions, and she couldn't decipher his thoughts. "He's not perfect, but he loves me. And you don't have to like him, because he's not your boyfriend. He's mine."

Reese stood up abruptly. "Let's go. I'll take you home."

They walked back to the SUV in silence and only said a few words to each other on the way to her apartment. When he pulled up in front of the hotel, she didn't wait for him to come around and open the door.

She hopped down from the vehicle and rushed inside.

CHAPTER 9

*A*nother friend getting hitched, which meant another event he had to attend. Reese sighed as he handed the valet his keys and headed toward the back of the stately manor where a garden party was taking place.

He straightened the lapels on his tan blazer as he strolled across the grass, smiling and nodding at acquaintances. Pockets of guests hovered near the refreshments while others congregated in groups, standing around or sitting at the tables set up all over the huge back yard. A cheer went up from the group of men playing bocce ball, while a few feet away four guests were having an intense political debate that included raised voices and plenty of rolled eyes.

The man and woman of the hour appeared before him and Reese came to a stop.

"Reese! My man."

Richard flung an arm around his shoulders. Both his parents ran hedge funds, and he was one of only a few Black students Reese went to school with. His future wife was short, blonde, and hailed from Sweden, though she'd lived in the country since she was five years old and didn't have an accent.

"Richard, what's up? Hi, Ingela," Reese said.

"Hello, Reese. It's good to see you."

He bent to give her a quick air-kiss, but she planted a real one at the corner of his mouth, on the side away from Richard. Reese stiffened and then quickly recovered, stepping back from her lingering lips. He'd always been uncomfortable in her presence, and that little stunt took him by surprise.

"Help yourself to anything you want," Ingela said. Because she stood in front of Richard, he couldn't see the way she eyed Reese with her suggestive comment.

"Your brother's over there." Richard pointed to where Stephan stood in the middle of a semi-circle, telling a story that had everyone laughing openly.

"Thanks."

Reese escaped and went over to where his brother held court. He tapped him on the shoulder, and Stephan stopped mid-sentence. When he saw Reese, his light brown eyes, which matched their mother's, widened. "Hey, look who's here. My little bro."

He knew that Reese hated when he said that but did it anyway. He finished telling the story and of course, everyone fell out laughing. Stephan had a good sense of humor and enjoyed being the life of the party. After Reese exchanged a few words with the rest of the group, the two brothers wandered away to talk privately.

"Where's Roselle?" Reese asked.

"She decided to skip this event. I can't blame her because I'm probably going to get out of here within a half-hour." He glanced at his watch, already counting down the time.

"I don't think I'm going to stay long, either. I just wanted to show my face."

"So, I heard you're still going to make a play for Nina?"

"Who told you that? Big-mouth Ella?"

Stephan chuckled. "Be nice. She saved our asses again with Mother. So, was she right?"

"Yeah. I'm making a play for Nina, boyfriend or no boyfriend." Though he'd screwed that up a little bit the last time they saw each other. Seemed every time he took one step forward with her, he took two steps back.

"You talked to Nina since the two of you had brunch on Sunday?"

Reese shook his head. "I called and left a message a couple of days ago to see if she was free any time this weekend, but I haven't heard back."

"Do you think—well, speak of the devil," Stephan murmured. He took a sip of punch and directed his gaze over Reese's right shoulder.

Following his brother's line of sight, Reese turned and saw Nina at one of two beverage tables set up in the yard. She wore a yellow and white horizontally striped dress that hugged her hips before the high-low hemline floated around her knees and the back of her calves. The sleeveless bodice showed off bare arms, and a wrist adorned with gold bangles.

Her normally thick, bouncy Afro was straightened, and her hair parted in the middle to lie in shiny loose waves around her face and on her shoulders. The sight of her elevated his spirits and destroyed his peace of mind at the same time.

Her eyes were perfection. Her nose was perfection. Her cheeks were perfection. She was perfection. No other woman before or after Nina had ever affected him so profoundly.

Suddenly, she laughed and did that cute little thing she always did where she wrinkled her nose in mock disgust. Reese would've kept his eyes on her regardless, but he definitely couldn't stop watching because she hadn't arrived alone. She came in on the arm of a dark-haired white-passing male. None other than Andy von Trapp. His father was white, his mother Black, but none of his features hinted at his biracial identity.

Reese never expected that seeing them would be this hard and suffered through the pain that arched through him. "Why'd she bring *him*?"

"He's her boyfriend, so it makes sense she'd bring him as a date," Stephan said.

"He shouldn't be here." His jaws locked so tight with tension, one would think they were wired shut.

"Says you. Don't cause a scene."

"I leave the scene-causing to you. I, on the other hand, am going over there to say hello."

"Whatever you're thinking, don't do it," Stephan warned.

Reese started toward them.

"Reese..."

He brushed off his brother's restraining hand and casually strolled to where the couple stood.

"Hi, Nina," he said.

Her eyes widened in surprise. "Hi, Reese."

"You get my message?"

"I, um, I did, but I didn't get a chance to call you back. I've been super-busy the past two days."

Yeah, right.

"Andy." Reese stuck out his hand.

"Do I know you?" Andy asked with a furrowed brow, shaking his hand.

Taken aback, Reese stared at him. He couldn't believe this guy was pretending he didn't know him. They might not be friends, but they went to the same school where Reese was a star athlete, and currently, they at least knew some of the same people.

"Reese Brooks. We went to Westerly Academy at the same time. My mother is Sylvie Johnson, who runs SJ Brands. Any of that ring a bell?"

Andy's face twisted into deep thought. "No, still doesn't," he said slowly.

The muscles in Reese's forearms bunched with the restraint needed not to slam Andy's head against the table. Maybe that would jog his memory.

Obviously sensing his annoyance, Nina jumped into the conversation. "Sylvie Johnson is the aunt to the Johnsons out of Seattle. You know, they make the number-one beer in the country at Johnson Brewing Company."

Reese watched as she gently stroked the other man's arm and, once again, his muscles tightened as he fought the over-whelming urge to slap away her hand. She should be touching him like that, not Andy.

Awareness sparked in Andy's eyes. "Oh, of course I know them. So you're a member of their family?"

"Cousins."

"Well, that's nice."

More than irritated, Reese decided to get under the other man's skin.

"Speaking of nice, you look great, Nina." He let his gaze travel over her shapely figure and the tempting cleavage revealed by the low neckline of the dress. He licked his lips. He couldn't help it. He could almost taste her breasts and the hard-ened nipples in his mouth, just like he could almost taste that kiss from over three years ago.

Nina's hand casually covered her chest, and that's when he realized he'd been staring. Her eyes begged him not to continue, but he ignored the silent plea.

"But you always do, don't you?" he added, biting his bottom lip.

A frown creased Andy's forehead and disappeared almost as quickly as it arrived. He rubbed up and down Nina's back. "Yes, she always looks fabulous."

Reese glared at his hand, then locked eyes with him. "You're a lucky man, Andy."

Andy stood a little taller, undoubtedly fully aware now that

Reese posed a threat. "Thank you. Don't I know it." He glanced between them, his gaze a little troubled. "How do you two know each other?"

"Nina and I met after a football game between Westerly and Springfield. I saw her in the stands and found her after the game, and we dated for a while."

"About a year and a half. A long time ago, but we're friends now." She smiled at Andy.

"I see. Well, it's nice to meet you, Reed."

"My name is *Reese*."

"Oh, excuse me. I'm terrible with names."

Was he smirking? This motherfu—

A solid hand landed on Andy's left shoulder. "Andy, my friend. We need to chat." Richard glanced at Nina. "Mind if I borrow him for a few minutes?"

"Not at all," Reese answered.

Nina shot him a look. "That's fine. Don't keep him too long."

"I'll bring him back right away."

Andy dropped a soft kiss to her lips, and Reese tensed at the display of intimacy. After Andy walked away with Richard, he met Nina's eyes.

"Your man is fucking disrespectful."

"Maybe he was following your lead," she said tartly. "I'm not in the mood for your macho act. Save it for your groupies."

"I don't have groupies."

She let her silence indict him.

"I don't," Reese insisted.

"Whatever. You were being a jerk." She turned away from him, and though her hair hid most of her face, he could see her jaw settle into hard lines.

"Was I?"

"Andy is a good guy," she said defensively. "You, however, are not. Are you proud of yourself?"

"I don't know what you're talking about."

She stepped closer and glanced over her shoulder, confirming that no one paid attention to them. "You know exactly what I'm talking about. That little stunt you pulled, paying me a compliment in front of him."

"What's the matter, he doesn't like it when you get compliments?" Damn, he wanted to kiss her right now. She was angry, but her rosebud lips were *right there* and presented such temptation.

"It's the way you said the words and the way you looked at me when you did."

He shrugged. "If your man is that insecure, maybe you shouldn't be together."

"He's not the one who's insecure," she said.

Reese laughed softly, though he wanted to find a wall to punch his fist through. Having her back in town should be a pleasant experience, but it only stressed him out. "Thought we were friends."

"Nothing has changed. You're the one making up new rules because... Because I don't even know why."

"Keep playing dumb," Reese said.

"I don't know what you're talking about."

"You know exactly what I'm talking about. You know how I feel."

"What do you want from me?"

"Everything. Everything we had."

"That's not possible."

"Because you refuse to acknowledge that there's still something between us. When I kissed you three and a half years ago, are you telling me you didn't feel anything?"

She stared at the small group playing bocce ball nearby and swallowed. "Nostalgia."

"That's it? Your panties didn't get wet?"

Her head whipped in his direction. "Don't talk to me like that!" she said in a fierce whisper.

"Why not? You like it too much?"

"Fuck you."

"Wish you would," Reese said, his voice filled with the hunger that consumed him from being mere inches from her and unable to touch.

As if he gave off too much heat, she stepped away and put more distance between them. He counted it a plus that she hadn't run off.

"Stop staring at me," Nina hissed.

"I'm staring?"

"You know you are."

"That's cause I'm hungry," Reese said in a low grumble.

Her breath hitched, proving she wasn't as indifferent as she pretended to be.

His eyes ate her up from bottom to top, but a glint on her finger snagged his attention. *What the...?*

Reese stopped breathing. He couldn't have been more out of breath if someone had snatched out his lungs.

"What's that?" he croaked.

Slowly, she looked down at her left hand as if seeing the piece of jewelry for the first time.

"An engagement ring," Nina said softly.

"An engagement ring? But that would mean..." He stared at her hand. "If that's an engagement ring..." he said, sounding strained. He could barely bring himself to accept the obvious. His chest hurt, and he felt as if he were having an out-of-body experience. "Th-that would mean you're engaged."

He lifted his eyes to hers.

"I am engaged. Two days ago, Andy asked me to marry him."

The ring glinted at him, mocking with its size and clarity. All he could think about was tossing her over his shoulder and taking her home, away from the man who'd placed himself between them—his new enemy.

"You're actually going to marry him? You're just running around getting engaged?"

"I'm not running around doing anything. I'm engaged. It's a thing people do. Not everyone wants to chase ass all their lives."

"You think that's what I do?"

"I know that's what you do. You'd just left some woman—or *women's*—bed when I saw you at The Winthrop less than a month ago. Give it a rest, Reese. We're done. Been done."

She almost walked away when he caught her wrist and switched his body in front of her, barring prying eyes from watching her during his interrogation.

"What are you doing?" he asked.

"Living my best life like I've always done. Now that includes getting engaged."

"You barely know him, Nina," he grated.

"I know him well enough. I've known him for over a year."

"You think I'm going to let this happen?"

"You don't get a say!"

"You're running from me."

"I am not running."

"Yes, you are, and we both know marrying him is not the answer. He's a poor substitute for me."

"God, you're arrogant! Could you stop for one minute and think about this from my point of view? Could you just be happy for me?"

"Would you be happy for me if I got engaged?" Reese could hardly breathe. The hold she had on him was indisputable and nerve-racking.

Her eyes flicked away from him, and several seconds passed before she answered. "Yes."

His heart squeezed with pain. "Then you're a better person than I am. But we already knew that, didn't we?"

She briefly closed her eyes and then opened them again. "Let me go, Reese." Her eyes dropped to where his fingers remained wound around her wrist. He tightened his hold for a second before reluctantly letting her go free.

Nina walked by him, and he turned slowly to see her take her place beside Andy. She was engaged. Wearing another man's ring.

Stephan came up beside him. "Easy, brother. You look like you want to kill someone."

His eyes remained on the woman he loved and then switched to the man she planned to marry. "Maybe I do."

CHAPTER 10

*A*ndy stretched his arms over his head as he walked to the mini-bar in Nina's apartment to make himself a drink. He'd insisted on coming over after they went out to dinner, but she'd hoped to sit with her own thoughts tonight.

"Can I fix you a drink?" he asked.

"No, I'm fine." She sat on the sofa and crossed her legs. Agitated since Richard and Ingela's party, she bounced her foot up and down. Not even the soothing creams and soft browns of the modern furniture could calm her nerves.

Unfairly, she kept replaying the conversation between Andy and Reese at the day party, and each time she found Andy lacking. As her boyfriend, Reese had never put up with another man coming onto her in his presence.

"You've been kind of quiet. You hardly said a word at dinner or on the way over here." Andy sat beside her on the sofa with a vodka on the rocks.

"I have a lot on my mind...work stuff. Dealing with the Helping Hands project, and of course, I don't feel prepared to take my father's place." She gave a little embarrassed laugh.

Andy's eyes filled with sympathy, and he reached over and

held her hand in his. "I hate to keep saying this, but taking over as CEO is not for you. Didn't you tell me you made some kind of mistake a while back that resulted in the firm losing a couple thousand dollars? It's not a lot, but it could've been worse if someone on your staff hadn't caught the mistake."

She had expected him to be supportive, not make her feel worse. Nina carefully withdrew her hand from his. "Not everyone is perfect and knows exactly what to do in every situation," she said defensively. She needed a boost of confidence, not a confirmation of her inadequacy.

"And for those of us who do, we're here to pick up the slack." He kissed her on the temple. "You know I love you, but you have to give yourself a break and stop worrying about things you can't control. Not everyone is programmed to be a CEO or an entrepreneur, and that's okay. Besides, what are you worried about? The company has run fine without your input for years, and once we're married, I'll make sure you never have to worry about anything except being a wife and mother. Let me deal with the stress of work and our security. That's *my* job as a man. And I want to take care of you. Okay?"

"Andy—"

"Love, listen to me. Just like when my parents married, our marriage will be the perfect synergy between two companies. Together, our holdings will total nearly a billion dollars, and I can only see us getting bigger from there. Stop worrying and let me take care of everything."

The conversation with Sylvie Johnson came to mind. "Are you saying you want me to be a housewife?" She hadn't expected him to lean toward old-fashioned roles in their relationship.

"I think it would be best, don't you? My mother never worked when we were children—not outside of the home, anyway. That came later."

73

"I don't want to be stuck at home while you're off, flying back and forth between New York and Atlanta."

"This is only temporary while we set up the Manhattan office."

"Is it?"

"Of course."

Nina played with the engagement ring, turning it around and around in a circle on her finger. "I don't want us to be strangers to each other. I want us both to be an influence in our children's lives."

"And we will be. I promise the schedule I have now is only temporary because I'm working hard with my father to learn the ropes while helping him set up our office in New York. There's a lot of work to do, tasks my mother handled when she was alive. Love, I'm not saying you have to sit at home doing nothing while our kids are at school. You could still have your charities and nonprofit work, but I think a merger between our two companies would be beneficial, and my father and I should handle The Winthrop for you since we both have more experience in the corporate world than you do." He patted her knee.

Disappointed, Nina stared down at her hands folded in her lap. Maybe he was right. Maybe she was in over her head.

"On another note, I have to agree with your friend, Reese. You looked particularly beautiful today."

She smiled at him. "Thank you."

"I prefer your hair like that—straight. My father likes it, too —did I mention that? I hope that's how you'll wear it for the wedding."

Nina touched her hair. "I hadn't really decided yet."

"Wear it straight," Andy said decisively. He laughed softly, in a patronizing way, before taking a sip of vodka.

She didn't mind switching up her look, but his comment unnerved her a bit. Reese liked her hair any way she fixed it— straight or curly, he always paid her compliments. With a sense of unease, she studied Andy. Since they'd been back, something was different. He didn't seem like the same man she had met in New Zealand.

Was it because he had to take on his responsibilities at the family business? Or because she kept comparing him, unfairly, to Reese?

Reese, who was also behaving differently. The ring should have put him off, but instead, he'd become more aggressive. He'd never been an angel, but the don't-give-a-shit part of his personality had been stripped bare at the party.

Andy set his glass on a coaster. "You know, there's something about Reese that bothers me. He gives off a vibe as if he still likes you. Maybe I'm wrong?" He looked at her expectantly, waiting for her to alleviate his concerns.

"We're friends," Nina said in a neutral voice.

"Was your relationship serious?"

They spent every free moment together before they went to different universities. Her parents had grown concerned about the intensity of their relationship, but they'd been young and in love. Inseparable. That's why she'd never suspected he could hurt her by saying they needed to break up. Then a mere week after their split, he slept with Kelly, of all people. Kelly, her nemesis. For some reason, she'd always been jealous of and disliked Nina and had hooked up with Nina's first boyfriend, Mark, when Nina wouldn't sleep with him. Nina had been called a prude for wanting to wait, so to have Reese hook up with the same girl had been like twisting a rusty blade in an old wound.

After they split, every morning had been a battle to get out of bed, yet because of her age, people dismissed her feelings. But she knew what she felt—a brutal sense of hurt and betrayal.

"Our relationship was a long time ago. We were teenagers, and he was my first..." Her gaze skittered away from his, and she shrugged.

"First what?" Andy pushed.

Nina straightened and faced him fully. "My first love, I guess." *And my first lover.*

"Any other former boyfriends lurking around the party that I need to know about?" he asked.

"Reese wasn't lurking." At his raised eyebrow, she hastily added, "And of course there weren't any other exes there. I would have told you. Look, you have nothing to worry about with Reese and me. We were young, foolish, and caught up in hormones. That's all in the past now."

Andy stroked his jaw, looking hard at her. "Completely over, right?"

She wouldn't mention the things Reese said to her or her own inexplicable desire for him. Besides, when would they run into each other again? Malik and Lindsay's wedding was over, and the garden party a fluke. She'd be careful about the places she went to because they knew the same people, but soon Reese would calm down, accept she'd moved on, and behave better when they saw each other.

"Completely over," Nina confirmed.

Andy stared at her, and she forced herself not to look away.

Finally, he gave her a kiss. "I'm going to take a shower."

When he disappeared, Nina slumped against the back of the sofa. Why did she feel so guilty when she hadn't done anything wrong? And would Reese really stop? Because the look in his eye suggested that not even a ring could stop him from coming after her.

CHAPTER 11

"**A**re you alone?" Reese's voice cracked like a whip.

Nina clutched the phone. "Yes. Why?"

"We need to talk."

"About what?"

"You'll find out soon enough."

"I don't want—"

"Open the door when I get there." He hung up.

Nina let out an angry scream in the middle of the empty room. Who did he think he was, making demands like that? She paced the floor with her arms crossed. How far away was he? She'd forgotten to ask—

Loud pounding made her jump. He must have been in the elevator. She hadn't had time to change out of the black shorts and tank top or release her hair from its freshly braided cornrows.

Oh, what the hell. Reese had seen her dressed casually plenty of times.

"Nina!"

She raced down the stairs and yanked open the door. "You don't have to yell."

"I didn't know if you'd open the door." His dark gaze swept over her body, pausing at her braless breasts before dropping lower to where the shorts clung to her hips and thighs. His angry expression shifted into something carnal and his nostrils flared, and now she really wished she'd changed.

Fighting the urge to cover her body, she demanded, "What do you want?"

The question snapped him out of the temporary trance, and he barged in and went into the living room.

Nina shut the door and followed, keeping a safe distance. He looked angry enough to chew through iron.

"You can't marry him."

"I figured you'd say that. Please, tell me why not."

"He's not right for you. I am."

"You? You told me a serious relationship was too much and unrealistic because we lived in different cities. You tossed my love back in my face."

"I didn't toss it back in your face. I panicked."

"And now you're ready, ten years later? No thanks, I'm not interested, and I'm not changing my mind."

"We both know you still have feelings for me. Doesn't that tell you something?"

"Yes, that I need to have my head examined."

"So, you admit you feel something." He seized on her admission with the quickness of a cat.

"Something, yes, but I don't know what that is. Nostalgia, probably."

"That's not nostalgia. You can deny your feelings all you want, but we both know they're real, and they're there. Damn it, Nina, how much longer are you going to punish me? I fucked up, I admit it, but it's been ten years. I didn't know Kelly hated you and slept with your first boyfriend."

She stepped away from him. "I'm not trying to hurt you. The decisions I make have nothing to do with you. They're for me.

Do you know how many people have told me to give you another chance? He's a good guy, they say, while you fly in women from all over, like a sultan with a harem.

"He made a mistake, they say. But *they* didn't have their heart ripped out." Her voice shook. "It's over. Accept it. Life would be so much easier for both of us if you do." She flashed her ring. "My life is with Andy."

"*No.*" The words were spoken through clenched teeth, sounding more like a snarl than a simple statement.

"I'm wearing his—"

"*No!*" His voice dropped sharp and hard, like a judge's gavel. "I will never accept that."

Nina took a quivering breath and spoke in a calmer voice. "I'm wearing his ring, Reese." Maybe if she kept saying the words, he'd finally accept them.

He briefly closed his eyes and then reopened them. "Take it off."

"I'm not doing this with you. I want you out of my house. Now." She jabbed a finger toward the door.

"I'm not leaving until I change your mind."

"Then I'll call security and have you kicked out."

"You won't do that."

She wouldn't, but she desperately wanted him to believe that she would.

They faced off against each other in the silence. Then Reese took her palm and pressed it to his lips. He sighed heavily, his shoulders dropping with the weight of emotion.

"You loved me once, you can love me again," he said softly.

With a little shiver, Nina dropped her gaze to the floor. The softness of his lips brought back so many memories. She should tug away, but she couldn't move. This was Reese, the man her younger self had thought she'd marry, grow old with, raise a family with.

Her greatest love. Her biggest mistake.

She shouldn't have allowed him to come in. Being alone with him conjured too many memories. More than friendly thoughts. Wild, dirty thoughts about his lips and hands and what he could do with them.

Silence strained the air between them, and she couldn't look at him. Not only because of what she would see in his eyes but what he would see in hers.

Wanting.

Aching.

A thirst unquenched for far too long.

His thumb gently stroked the inside of her wrist. A light, almost careless touch that nonetheless sent a spark of fire tearing through her blood.

Her fingers on that same hand started to tremble. She needed to pull away—anything but let him continue to touch her.

Reese eased closer and caressed up her arm past her elbow to her shoulder. His touch shouldn't feel so good. She shouldn't want him so much. She shouldn't want him to do more than touch her arm.

"Look at me, Nina," he whispered.

She briefly closed her eyes to gain the strength needed to resist him. When she finally looked at him, that newfound strength evaporated like steam. She became lost in his gaze and opened her mouth to beg him to stop. To leave her be, because she couldn't resist him. Not now. Maybe not ever.

Because as soon as he pushed against her boundaries just a little bit, reached for more than friendship, the walls she'd erected would shatter like brittle ceramic.

He pulled her closer, lifting a hand to the side of her neck. "I missed you like crazy. So many times I wanted to get on a plane and go to wherever you were. I waited to give you room. Don't tell me my waiting was in vain."

He lowered his head a few inches, mouth hovering over hers.

She could almost hear the time ticking slowly past.

His head dipped lower, and their lips touched. Nina released a soft whimper at the tail end of a shaky breath. Mentally and physically, she succumbed to the intense attraction that flared to life between them.

Reese tilted her head back as his tongue flicked against the seam of her lips, and the same hand that cradled her neck pulled her closer. With that slight encouragement, she curled her fingers into the front of his shirt using a tight clasp, as if letting go meant she risked losing her hold on him.

But Reese clearly wasn't going anywhere. His mouth moved over Nina's in a devouring motion, plucking at her lips and nibbling at the corners of her mouth.

The possessive kiss declared his ownership of her—as if she'd never stopped belonging to him during the entirety of the past ten years.

Reese slid his hands down her back and over her bottom, kneading each ass cheek while his searching mouth teased her with kisses that left her trembling on tiptoe and panting for more.

Cradling her bottom in his hands, he lifted her from the floor and walked to the sofa, their lips never once losing contact in the all-consuming kiss.

Reese eased her onto her back and settled firmly between her thighs. His erection lined up with precision against her core, and she shivered at the delicious sensations that pulsated through her lower abdomen from the point of contact. Grinding his hips as if he was already fucking her, he handed out a sample of what he'd do if black shorts and dark jeans didn't keep them from skin-to-skin contact.

She came alive with sensation, breathless with anticipation and aching with longing and need. What would it be like to be taken by him? To lie totally naked and succumb to mind-numbing pleasure.

She kissed him harder and moved restlessly. His mouth lowered to her throat, and Nina arched backward so he could cover more surface. One hand smoothed up her belly under the tank top, igniting heat like a lit torch had been set to her skin. His fingers splayed out against her stomach and then squeezed her waist. His attack on her was gentle but unrelenting, and in the midst of this, his hips continued a slow-motion grind between her legs.

He scattered kisses on her neck and collarbone while that wayward hand at her waist eased lower and finally squeezed the throbbing flesh between her legs. Nina sucked air between her teeth and curled her fingers into the soft cushion of the sofa. The shock of what he'd done stripped away her ability to remain calm.

"You still taste the same, don't you?" he rasped. His head went lower, and he kissed the tips of her breasts through her top.

Nina watched with half-closed lids as he pushed her shirt higher and licked her bared belly.

"I know you do," he whispered shakily.

She watched with combined horror and anticipation as he kissed her hips and upper thighs over her clothes. With each caress of his lips, her inhibitions crumbled.

She half-heartedly pushed at his shoulders, trying so very hard to be strong.

One hand found her right breast while the thumb of his other hand played with her needy clit. Instead of closing her legs or pushing him away, Nina spread her thighs wider and listened to his satisfied groan as she submitted to his touch. He continued to stroke, and of its own accord, her pelvis undulated with each movement of his hand.

Stop! Her mind screamed, but the words never left her lips. Reese whispered something that sounded like, "Let me get a taste."

She knew what he was about to do, and for a reckless moment, her open thighs went lax to accommodate him. To let him have his way. To be at his mercy and do what he wanted and do what she needed with every fiber of her being.

"No," she whispered, a lame effort to refuse him that he couldn't hear past his own heavy breathing.

She trembled on the edge of surrender, and then he mashed his face between her legs, and she almost came from the impact. Grabbing the back of his head, she moaned and arched her back. Her panties were sopping wet and damn near dripping with the evidence of her desire. The hands holding her legs open tightened as he dragged his moist tongue along the inside of her thigh toward its target.

But then a framed photo on a side table came into focus—a selfie she and Andy took on a beach in Australia. And just like that, she couldn't. She found her voice and one word to stop him.

"No!"

The louder exclamation caught his attention, and he lifted his head, his dark eyes holding a drugged appearance.

"What's wrong?"

"I don't want to. I can't." She sounded panicked because that's how she felt. What was she doing? *You love Andy—not Reese* repeated in her head, like a broken record.

Confusion filled his eyes as if he couldn't comprehend her words. But he sat up, and Nina shimmied backward to escape. She jumped up from the sofa and stood a safe distance away, breathing hard, and so was Reese. The bulge in his pants made his desire as plain as her wet panties.

Nina ran her tongue over her swollen, throbbing lips. "Why did you do that?" she asked in a shaky voice.

"Why did you let me?"

She covered her face with both hands. Her nipples still ached for his touch. "God, Reese, what happened just now was wrong, and you know it."

He stood angrily. "You think I give a damn about wrong or right where he's concerned? You belong with me. That's all I care about."

"You are so damn selfish. You haven't changed."

"I'm selfish for what's mine."

"I don't belong to you."

"Lies, and you know it. What just happened was intense, and you didn't want me to stop." He came closer. "And I didn't want to stop."

"I am with Andy."

"You don't even love him."

"Yes, I do!"

"Then say it. Tell me you love him."

"I love him."

"Say it like you mean it. I don't believe you."

"You'll never believe me because it's not what you want to hear!" she screamed, shaking.

Reese spoke calmly, enunciating every word. "I don't believe you because it's not true. You're it for me, and I know I'm it for you, too. We can go back to where we were before, with all the excitement and passion that we had when we were young. It's still there. I felt it just now."

She blinked rapidly to stem the flow of tears that threatened to fall. "We were kids. I'm a woman now, and I...I'm with someone else. You have to accept my engagement. You have to, or—" she swallowed "—or I'll cut you from my life. I can't let you kiss me, and I can't let you say those things to me anymore. It's disrespectful to Andy. So please stop, or I... We can't be friends anymore."

"I don't want to be your friend. It's not enough anymore. It never was."

"That's what *you* wanted. You made the decision to break up with me, and you made the decision to sleep with Kelly. But you can't handle that truth because it makes you uncomfortable."

"I'm not uncomfortable. I'm tired. You think I haven't suffered enough? When does this end? All these years you've been dangling yourself like a carrot in front of me."

Her eyes widened. "I have not!"

"Yes, you have. You already got me back. You cut me off for over a year."

Nina stepped back from him. He had no idea how she'd suffered over the course of that year. What she'd been through. "We keep hurting each other. It's not healthy," she said in a dull voice.

"If it means being away from you, I don't want to be healthy."

Folding her arms protectively over her stomach, the memory she'd pushed down the farthest resurfaced. "Kelly's not the only reason I left that night."

"There was no one else, I swear to you, and it was just that one time. I never touched her again."

She remained silent, staring at the floor.

His hands encircled her arms, and he forced her to look at him. "Nina, you have to believe me. I wanted you back the minute you came to the party. There was no one else and no other times."

The desperation in his voice prompted her to speak. "I know."

Confusion coated his features. "Then what are you talking about? What else happened?"

She took a deep breath and let it ease past her lips. "The reason I showed up at your house that night was because I had something important to tell you. I came to tell you…to tell you that I was pregnant."

CHAPTER 12

*R*eese blinked once, then twice. "What?"

Nina withdrew from his touch and, numb with shock, he let her go.

"I came to tell you that I was pregnant. I didn't know you were having a party, and I almost changed my mind. I knew the week before and chickened out after you said you didn't want to be with me anymore. I had to finish what I'd come there to do, but I needed to work up the courage. It helped that you seemed so happy to see me." She laughed a little, but the laughter was mixed with pain. "Then Kelly showed up, and you started acting so weird. I still intended to tell you. I was waiting for the right time. Maybe after everyone left...I don't know. But before I could, Kelly cornered me and told me what happened between the two of you."

Damn it, Kelly. He wished he'd never touched her.

"That's why you cut me off."

She nodded. "I was hurt at first, but then after I started to show, I couldn't let you see me. I was sick a lot, too, while I was pregnant. It was a tough time, so that's why I didn't go back to college in the fall."

Reese needed to sit, but couldn't move. His knees might not support the walk to the sofa. "What happened to our...to our baby?"

Nina hugged herself and directed the words to the floor. "I miscarried two months later."

He wanted to reach out and touch her but wasn't sure he should. "Boy or girl?" His voice sounded strange—tight, like being forced to speak around a chokehold.

"A boy," she whispered.

He'd never pined for children the way other people did. As a matter of fact, he'd never wanted any at all, but at that moment —in the midst of learning that he had almost become a father— an ache twisted inside him with such force he froze. He was almost a father, and Nina would have been the mother of his child.

Reese staggered over to the sofa, sank into the soft cushion, and buried his face in his hands. "You should have still told me."

"Why?"

He lifted his head. "Because I deserved to know."

"Do you have any idea how I felt coming to you with that news after you told me you didn't want me, knowing you didn't want kids on top of that? Then I found out about Kelly. How was I supposed to let you know about a baby when you'd already moved on after one lousy week? I wasn't thinking about you, I was thinking about how I would get through that pregnancy."

If he had ever needed proof that they were over, this was it. Her body wanted him, but her heart and mind did not. No matter her reason, she left his house without giving the slightest hint that she'd been carrying his child. Then she lost the baby and still never uttered a word.

While the littlest smile from her spread sunshine through his heart, he clearly brought only dark skies filled with storm clouds into hers.

"You were going to cut me out. You were never going to tell me, were you?" he said.

"I don't know. I would have, eventually. But right then, I couldn't."

Reese stood, his body weighed down with the heaviness of his thoughts and what he'd just learned. "Does he really make you happy?" he asked, finding it difficult to form the words.

Nina twisted the ring on her finger in one full circle. He waited for her answer with nerves stretched as taut as primed guitar strings.

"Yes," she said quietly.

No word had ever pained him more.

Adding to his regret for his actions, he now could add the loss of their unborn baby. How would their lives have changed if she'd told him what she came over that day to say? He'd never know. There were no sliding doors to show their life in an alternate universe.

"Good. You deserve to be happy."

The lump in his throat was so unbearably thick, he almost choked on the words. He dropped his gaze. All he wanted was for her to be happy. No, that was a lie. He wanted to be the one to make her happy. It would break his heart to see her happily married to someone else.

He snatched up the keys he'd tossed on the table when he arrived and went to the door in a rush to escape. He couldn't look at her anymore, knowing she'd never be his again. Knowing she'd suffered through a miscarriage alone because she couldn't trust him and didn't believe in him. And now she'd have kids with the man she was going to marry, who wasn't him. His behavior had caused that.

To him, their togetherness was as inevitable as the shifting of night into day. Hope had kept him going all this time—hope he still had a chance, and they'd one day reconcile, but he knew now that wasn't the case. His hopes had been nothing but wishful thinking.

Just accept it, a mocking voice whispered.

He rushed down the stairs to the front door.

"Reese..." her voice cracked. "We can still...I mean, our friendship doesn't have to end." She half-whispered the words as if she knew friendship status was insufficient.

He paused without turning. "I don't want to be your friend, Nina." He continued out the door.

If he'd known then what he knew now—that he would be sentenced to life without Nina—he would have never set her aside. He would have never slept with Kelly.

Then he wouldn't have to endure this life-long sentence.

* * *

NINA CURLED up in the bed and squeezed her eyes shut. Cutting all ties was for the best. The hole in her heart had healed enough for her to forget and function while overseas, but if Reese remained in her life, he would disrupt her plans, and she'd eventually start picking at the scab. She couldn't allow herself to be vulnerable to him again.

The phone rang, and she snatched it up—for one second thinking it might be Reese. Andy's name flashed on the screen, but she didn't have the energy to talk to him right now. She flipped the phone over on its face and let the call go to voice mail.

Her eyes shuttered closed as she relived the episode in the living room. The best thing that had happened to her body in a long time was having Reese put his hands and mouth anywhere he pleased. It had been so long since she felt that way, desire barreling through her like an eighteen-wheeler. She would have to take her shameful actions to the grave, just like she would have to accept the end to their friendship.

If she hadn't kissed him, he would have stayed firmly in the friend zone. The kiss gave him hope. But at least now he knew the truth. She didn't just lose him, she lost their baby, too.

And deep down she knew, if she dared give an honest self-evaluation, she had never fully recovered from the loss of either.

CHAPTER 13

Spending the Fourth of July on the beach in the Golden Isles off the coast of Georgia was not originally on Reese's list of things to do. Still, when his mother called and insisted he participate, he reluctantly agreed.

Oscar had wanted a "normal" holiday celebration, so Sylvie rented three houses on the beach for all of them. His parents stayed in the smaller one with Trevor, who'd come on the trip, too. Stephan and his family, Reese, and Malik and Lindsay occupied the one next door. On the other side of that one was where Ella and Simone and their spouses and children slept.

His mother had suggested he bring a friend, but he'd declined. Who would he call? There was no one he was interested in bringing around his family.

St. Simons Island was the largest island in the chain, and its untouched beauty made for a lovely escape from the city. Large oaks dripping with moss lined the streets, and with quaint shops, museums, golf courses, and the pristine waters of the Atlantic Ocean lapping at the white sand, there was plenty to do.

Reese stood on the beach in a pair of swim trunks, his open

shirt allowing the gentle breeze to brush his exposed chest, a half-empty can of beer in hand. Unfortunately, he had the debatable pleasure of watching the happy family units comprised of his siblings and cousin, enjoying the beach, which brought stark attention to his singleness. As odd man out, he began to think he should leave early and save himself the misery.

"You can't turn the meat from way back there, Sylvie," his father said in an annoyed voice.

Reese glanced over his shoulder. Both his parents stood behind the huge grill, quite an interesting sight to see.

"I'm *trying*, Oscar," his mother said, though she didn't look like she was trying at all, holding a metal spatula aloft in one hand and a glass of white wine in the other. She wrinkled her nose as she backed away from the cooking meat, whose tempting aroma filled the air, thanks to Oscar's secret blend of herbs and spices. Sylvie bumped into his father, who stood behind her. "It's just so *hot*."

His father had convinced her not to bring a full staff like she often did on family trips. Only Trevor had come along to help Oscar and Simone's husband Cameron, who liked to cook, to make sure all the meals were prepared. But at this rate, they wouldn't be eating for a couple more hours, and Reese was already starving. Trying to teach Sylvie domestic skills was a complete waste of time because his mother—who had spent her entire life with servants at her beck and call, thus avoiding doing any work in the kitchen—was not about to change. She didn't even look the part.

Oscar was casually dressed in long swim trunks and a light gray T-shirt, while she looked ready to do a fashion shoot in an electric blue one-piece under a white cover-up cinched at the waist. On her head, she wore a huge white hat with an electric blue band around the crown, which hid half her face but showed enough for you to see her high cheekbones and catch a glimpse of piercing brown eyes when she cocked her head at the right angle. He was pretty sure she had no intention of getting in the water.

Oscar took the spatula. "What am I going to do with you?"

"Keep me," Sylvie said, glancing back at him with a mischievous grin. She angled her cheek upward for him, her usual move to let the men in her life know that she expected a kiss.

Oscar slid an arm around her waist and instead of kissing her cheek, kissed her neck.

"Oscar, for heaven's sake," she said, letting loose a burst of girlish giggles.

They were sickening, but in a good way. Reese turned away from the sight, feeling as if he were a Peeping Tom. Most of the time, they seemed so happy, he wondered if their fifteen-year split had actually made their current relationship stronger. They had fallen back into the natural order of things, seamlessly transitioning into an affectionate couple. Too bad that couldn't happen for him and Nina.

Sylvie appeared beside him and placed a gentle hand on his back. "Hello, my darling. Are you all right?" She angled her head so he could see her concerned gaze under the large hat.

"Fantastic," Reese lied.

"You're having a good time?"

"Sure. The whole family's here."

She studied him in silence, her shrewd gaze traveling over his face. "What's wrong?"

"Nothing, Mother." He tried to laugh off her concern, but it ended up sounding hollow and empty.

"Tell me what's wrong and don't deny it again, because I know you."

Reese huffed out a breath. She was too perceptive. "Nina and I are done."

"Done?" Sylvie said sharply. "What does that mean?"

He dented one side of the can with his thumb. "Our friendship has come to an end."

"For heaven's sake, Reese, we had a lovely brunch just last month. What happened?"

"She and I had a fight, and..."

I was pregnant.

She never saw fit to tell him. Did she really think that he was such an awful person? Did she hate him that much? Even worse, had he caused her such emotional distress that she lost their baby? The possibility had haunted him ever since he learned about the miscarriage.

He'd have a son about nine years old if the child had lived, and his chest hurt for what could have been. He felt wide open, raw. If touched, he would feel the pain all the way to the bottom of his heart.

Marriage and kids had never been in the cards for him, but for Nina, he would have made the leap.

"The reason she and I had a fight doesn't matter. We're done, and I'd appreciate it if you don't mention her name in my presence ever again. No more comments about how she's your ex-future daughter-in-law."

"Well, of course, you know I wanted her as a daughter-in-law and the mother of my grandchildren."

Reese winced internally. "Mother."

"Yes, I know. Your friendship is over. That was quite a fight."

"It was." Reese took another sip of beer, letting his gaze travel over the four people playing in the waves—his sister, Ella, her two daughters, and their stepfather, Tyrone.

"Are you all right?"

"I will be. I just need you to do that for me." He met her gaze again.

"I will do whatever you need."

"Thank you," he said gratefully. Then he remembered part of the conversation at brunch that had given him pause. "When

Nina was at your place, why did you make that comment about it being quite a coincidence that she ran into Andy in New Zealand?"

Sylvie smiled knowingly. "Because I don't believe in coincidences."

She had seen ugliness from people who let greed direct their moral compass, and she ran businesses in the cutthroat industries of media and fashion. All of which made her naturally suspicious, sometimes without cause.

But...was there something suspicious about Andy running into Nina on that farm in New Zealand? He couldn't be sure. He would analyze his mother's concerns more deeply another day. Right now, enough about Nina.

In an effort to change the subject, he angled his head toward his father. "How did you like grilling?"

"I hated it. I hope your father never puts me behind that dreadful thing again." She shivered and took a sip of wine.

"Did you at least turn one hamburger?"

Sylvie shot him a look. "I run a multibillion-dollar corporation, darling. I do not turn hamburgers. I don't know why your father insists on these little experiments. I am who I am, and I'm not going to change."

Reese chuckled softly.

"Why are you laughing?" Sylvie asked, arching one elegant eyebrow higher.

He placed an arm around her shoulders and squeezed. "Because I love you, Mother. I don't want you to change."

She beamed at him. "I love you, too, and I won't. Don't you worry about that."

"Coming through!"

Cameron Bennett, Simone's husband, came out of Oscar and Sylvie's house. He carried covered containers in his hands, and Simone and Trevor followed behind him with more.

"Please tell me that's food," Reese said.

Cameron grinned. The guy loved to cook, and that grin was definitely a good sign.

"Appetizers are served," Simone announced. Since marrying Cameron, she'd developed a love for cooking.

Within minutes, Roselle came from inside the house next door, where she had gone to check on her daughter. Stephan, who'd been lounging on a beach chair waiting for her to return, jumped up as Ella and her family came running up from the beach.

There was spinach dip served alongside a crudité platter, deviled eggs—half topped with fish roe and the other with smoked salmon—and shrimp in crispy wonton cups with spicy mayo served on the side.

Sylvie prepared a plate for Oscar and kept him company while the rest of them crowded around the table and indulged in the pre-dinner snacks Simone, Cameron, and Trevor had prepared.

"Mmm, this is tasty," Sophia, Ella's eldest daughter, said. Her fair complexion had darkened after a day of fun on the beach. She swirled a carrot stick into some of the dip Ella had spooned onto her plate and then bit down hard on the vegetable. The crunching sound made her giggle exactly like it did the two other times she did the same thing.

The appetizers hit the spot and held them over until the rest of the food was served an hour later. The meal consisted of a briny corn, tomato, and red cabbage salad, bacon-wrapped potatoes, and cilantro-lime chicken. A makeshift burger bar set up on a folding table allowed everyone to prepare theirs the way they preferred.

For the rest of the evening, they simply enjoyed each other's company. Malik showed pictures of his latest metal sculpture creation. Tyrone kept them entertained with stories from his days in law enforcement, and Cameron did the same with tales from his adventures as a night club owner. Hannah, Ella's younger daughter, insisted on sitting on her Poppa's lap, eating more off Oscar's plate than her own, and Sylvie recounted embarrassing stories from her two daughters' childhood that had their husbands howling with laughter.

Despite the mess with Nina, Reese looked around the table and felt a surge of happiness. Along with Trevor, his big family filled two tables out on the beach, talking and laughing and lingering over their meal as the day succumbed to night, and the lanterns set up around them kept the shadows at bay.

He recognized how lucky he was and how much he'd needed this trip. They ate too much. They drank too much. They laughed too much.

He was glad he'd come after all.

CHAPTER 14

*H*er mother was in her element.

Nina smiled wryly as Gloria Winthrop rubbed elbows with the wealthy patrons in attendance at the annual fundraiser. The top of the black dress crossed over her ample bosom, and her short black wig gave the opportunity to show off the diamonds in her ears that matched the ones around her wrist. She laughed at the appropriate times, shot friendly waves across the room, and in general, looked like she was having a good time without being disrespectful about the gravity of tonight's subject matter. Gloria may not have been born into wealth, but she'd made a seamless transition into the lifestyle.

Nina was reasonably sure she'd married her father for his money, and when his priorities and hers didn't match, the marriage fell apart. He'd loved her during the marriage and after the divorce, but he'd wanted her to change—to see their wealth as an opportunity, yes, but not have it consume their lives.

When was enough, enough? Though he'd provided for her in his will, Gloria was not satisfied and often asked Nina for more money or possessions, none of which she seemed capable of getting enough of.

From her chair at one of the head tables, Nina searched the room of donors. Her father would be pleased to see how far the event had come since his passing. The annual art fundraiser to benefit victims of domestic violence wasn't the most well-known of the many galas and fundraisers that made the social calendar each year. Still, it had gained prestige in the past few years since sexual harassment, rape, and domestic violence became more prominent in the news cycle. Nina attended and threw her support behind the cause, not only because of its importance to her as a woman but because her father had wanted her to.

Tyrus Winthrop had earmarked a percentage of his estate to make annual contributions to his favorite charities after his death, and this was one of them. After seeing his mother wither under abuse at the hands of his stepfather for years, he'd vowed to do whatever he could to help other women, and did so throughout his life, funding programs that provided emotional, financial, and educational support.

Nina hadn't been able to attend any of the fundraisers in recent years because of her travel outside of the country, but she always made sure the donations were forwarded as her father had wanted.

"How much longer do we have to be here?" Andy asked, looking restless as he tugged on his tie for the umpteenth time.

Nina bristled at his tone. She bristled a lot more these days because she hadn't expected this type of behavior from a man who'd worked with her on various projects for more than a year. Glancing at him, she could see he seemed distracted and wondered if his father was overworking him. She should be more sympathetic. Act more like a fiancée.

She gently covered his hand with hers to stop the fidgeting. "Not much longer. There are a few other people I'd like to meet before we leave."

"Thirty minutes, maybe?" Andy asked hopefully, stretching his hand along the back of her chair.

She smiled indulgently at him. "Yes, thirty minutes."

"Thanks." He kissed her cheek.

"On one condition. We have to stop for ice cream on the way home."

"You really love ice cream, don't you?" he said with a little laugh.

"It's my favorite dessert, and you know why," she said teasingly.

This entire conversation was odd, considering one of the ways they'd bonded overseas was by seeking out the best ice cream and gelato in the various places they visited. But surely he understood it wasn't just the ice cream that she liked, but what the cold treat represented.

"Because of your father." His voice sounded heavy, as if the topic of her father had become tiresome to him.

"Are you trying to tell me something?" Nina asked, choosing to keep her gaze trained on a door across the room so he wouldn't see the displeasure in her face.

"I don't think you can continue living your life for someone who's passed away, that's all. You want to run the business because of him. You do volunteer work because of him. You love ice cream because of him. It's...a lot."

Nina squelched down her fury with a deep breath. She faced Andy, refusing to hide her displeasure this time. "He was my father and my best friend. I adored him and his mind and his generosity. I'm disappointed you can't understand that."

He appeared startled but quickly fixed his face into an expression of contrition and placed a placating hand on her far shoulder. "I'm acting like an ass, but it's because I'm ready to get you out of here and get you home, that's all." He lowered his voice at the end and stroked his fingers along the nape of her bare neck.

She wore her hair swept up to the top of her head in a neat ball secured with pins. With an emerald green dress showing off her shoulders, she looked the part of a wealthy young socialite. Andy looked the part of her dashing partner in a simple black suit and tie, his dark hair parted on the side and swept over to the right.

Yet his comments reminded her of how the most supposedly cultured people could have the manners and eloquence of swine.

"I'm going to get a drink," she said, standing.

Andy frowned up at her. "Okay."

Nina left the table, perturbed by his lack of understanding about her relationship with her father. Were they already drifting apart?

Reese would have jumped at the chance to get ice cream with her, though he limited himself to only three flavors. He also knew about and understood her relationship with her father and never commented on their closeness—not even when he knew that he'd fallen out of favor with Tyrus.

As she approached the bar, she wondered what he was doing now. She'd wished she could call him to discuss her tweaks to The Winthrop Helping Hands program and share the timeline for the rollout. Reese would be happy for her instead of the lukewarm reaction she'd received from Andy, who had burst her bubble by questioning whether the data was correct.

Nina ordered a chocolate martini, and as she took a sip, she spotted Sylvie Johnson nearby in conversation with a tall man.

A split second later, Sylvie noticed her, too, and smiled. She then excused herself and came over.

"Hello, Ms. Johnson, I had no idea you were here tonight."

"I only just arrived."

"Is Mr. Brooks here, too?"

"Yes, over there," she replied with a nod of her head. Across the room, Oscar chatted with one of the organizers. "And who are you here with?"

"My mother and...and Andy." She had hesitated over his name, unsure if she should mention him or not.

"Ah, yes, your fiancé. There he is." Sylvie's eyes narrowed slightly on Andy. "We spent a lovely Fourth on St. Simons Island. I wish you could have joined us."

"That would not have been possible."

"Because of your fiancé?"

"Partially, but also because Reese and I had a falling-out."

"He told me, and I was so sorry to hear that. I do hope the two of you can work things out. You've known each other for so long, after all. Since you were practically children."

"Time will tell," Nina murmured.

She did miss him. Reese had always sort of been there whether she needed him or not. Not being able to pick up the phone and hear his voice was unexpectedly distressing.

Sylvie slipped her jeweled clutch between her waist and elbow. "Step this way, please. I'd like to say something to you."

Uh-oh.

Nina's hand tightened around the stem of her glass, but she followed anyway to a far wall.

Sylvie looked her directly in the eyes, not in an antagonistic way, but with kindness in her eyes.

"My children consider me a busybody, and perhaps I am. But what mother isn't? No matter their age, we always want to help and fix our children's problems." Her stare became more intense. "This is me trying to fix the problem between you and Reese."

Nina swallowed.

"His father and I split for a long time, as you know. Sometimes time away from the person you love is good. At least it was for Oscar and me. It clears your head. Especially when you hurt each other. It just makes more sense to take a break before coming together again. I don't spend as much time with my children anymore, because they all have busy lives. They're all adults. But I know them. I raised good people. I know their hearts. Reese loves you."

"Ms. Johnson—" Nina started.

Forcing her into silence with a squeeze on her arm, Sylvie continued. "It's not a secret, Nina. You know he loves you. You'd have to blind not to know that all these years he's carried a torch for you. Love can make you do crazy things. Run toward it, run away from it out of fear. I know the reason he broke up with you, but he loves you. He was young, foolish, impulsive— all of those things. Wrong. Selfish. Idiotic. All of those things, too. But he does love you. I want the two of you back together, but I'm his mother. Of course, I do. I want him to be happy, and he's not happy without you. But you also need to make the decision that's right for *you*. The decision that makes you most happy. I believe you're most happy with my son."

Nina boldly faced the woman she admired. "With all due respect, I don't believe you understand how incompatible Reese and I are. We're better off as friends, and if we can't be friends, then…"

She swallowed hard. The thought of him never being a part of her life ever again—even in a friendship role—was hard to fathom.

Sylvie smiled slowly, knowingly. "We make decisions based on our life experiences. As individuals, we see the world through different lenses. Do not make a decision about the rest of your life based on consensus or what other people deem right or wrong or acceptable."

She paused to let the words sink in.

"You owe Reese nothing, and the two of you may never speak again. But if you marry this *Andy*…" She emphasized his name in a disparaging way as if those two syllables soiled her tongue. "Make sure you do so for the right reasons. Because when you're with the one you love—" She glanced to where her husband stood and then returned her gaze to Nina. "It's the best feeling in the world. There truly is nothing better."

Nina straightened her spine. "Thank you, but I know what I'm doing."

"Do you? You're young, you're rich, you're idealistic. A word of advice: beware of wolves in sheep's clothing, Nina. Sometimes the wolves are much closer than you think."

What did that mean? "Are you suggesting that Andy—"

Gloria came to stand next to Nina and gave Sylvie a venomous look that let her know in no uncertain terms that she wished she were not there.

"Sylvie," Gloria said coolly by way of greeting.

"Gloria," Sylvie said, with equal frost.

Neither woman seemed capable of exchanging pleasantries.

There had always been tension between them, and not long ago, Nina learned why. Lindsay divulged a secret their mother had been hiding for years. Lindsay had read Gloria's journal and discovered that she'd had her heart broken by none other than Cyrus Johnson—Sylvie Johnson's older brother—when he married another woman.

"I hope you're not filling my daughter's head with nonsense."

Sylvie gave a short, airy laugh. "Me? Of course not, Gloria. I leave that distasteful task to you." While Gloria quietly seethed, Sylvie gave Nina a fond smile. "Have a lovely evening, my darling, and remember what I said." She went in the direction of her husband.

"I can't stand that old bitch," Gloria muttered.

"Mom!" Nina exclaimed in a mortified whisper.

"She's horrible. She thinks she's better than everyone else and is so damn fake. Always with her 'my darling' this and 'my darling' that. And what exactly did she mean by that last remark, anyway? What do you need to remember?"

Sylvie sidled up to her husband as she joined him to chat with the organizer.

Nina turned away. "Nothing important." She took a sip of her chocolate martini.

Gloria's eyebrows lowered over her eyes. "Are you sure?"

"I'm positive." A blatant lie, because Sylvie had reminded her of a niggling question that she'd wondered about ever since brunch at her home.

Tonight she would ask the question and insist on getting an answer.

CHAPTER 15

*H*is body language gave him away.

Andy's eyes widened slightly, and his shoulders stiffened as if he were going into defense mode, fingers frozen on the knot in his tie in the middle of tugging it from around his neck.

Nina had wanted an unguarded reaction. That's why she had asked the question so abruptly, throwing it at him with no warning in the middle of his bedroom as he began to undress.

"Did you or did you not arrange the meeting with me in New Zealand? Meeting me wasn't a coincidence, was it?" she asked in a harder voice.

He kept busy removing his tie. "What made you ask me that out of the blue?"

"Answer the question, Andy," Nina commanded, though she had already guessed the answer.

Their whole "accidental" meeting had been planned. So much for kismet. So much for the notion of Fate stepping in to bring her a man who was safe.

"Nina, listen to me." Andy's eyes held urgency as he came toward her, reaching.

She sidestepped him. "Answer the question."

Running his fingers through his dark hair, Andy let his shoulders drop. His body language signaled his deception, but he wouldn't vocalize it.

"How could you?"

His face crumbled in distress before clearing so quickly she almost thought she'd imagined the pained expression.

"Do you want to know the truth? I had my eyes on you for a long time, and I didn't know how to approach you. Then I heard you'd left the country, and I panicked. I had to do something to get your attention."

"Was anything you told me the truth? About your favorite color being green like mine, or that you have the same desire to make a difference in the world…?" Her voice trailed off because she read his expression and the clear truth. "All lies?" she whispered.

"Not all. I do admire your work and want to change the world with you. That's something we can do as a married couple."

"But philanthropy was never your calling, was it?"

"No," he admitted in a low voice.

"We spent a year and a half doing all that work. Did you enjoy what you did?"

"Some, but not most," he admitted reluctantly.

"So you were being fake. You're not the person I thought you were."

"There are a few differences from the man I presented myself to be, but I'm the same man. A man who loves you and admires you. I am the man who thinks you're beautiful and caring, and unlike any woman I've ever met. I'm the man you fell in love with and agreed to marry."

"Do you really want kids? Do you really want to have a family?" His answers were terribly important to her. A deal breaker if he answered in the negative.

"Of course. And I want those things with you."

Andy walked over slowly, tentatively, as if he suspected Nina would reject him. She searched his face and wondered if she'd made another mistake.

Andy stopped inches away and cupped her shoulders. "The way I went about winning your heart was not totally honest, but my intentions were pure. I knew you were the woman for me."

Conflicted, Nina stepped away, and his hands fell to his sides.

"I don't know how I feel right now," she said.

He swallowed. "I understand, but please don't leave me. Don't throw away everything we've shared over the past year and a half because of a few..."

"*Lies?*" she supplied since he seemed reluctant to say the word.

He winced. "Nina, we've had plenty of good times and can have many more. We can get past this."

She sure knew how to pick men. The two men she'd loved had deceived her. First, Reese had made her fall in love with his charm and good looks. Then he'd broken her heart by insisting he wasn't ready to be in a serious relationship and rubbed salt in the wound by sleeping with a woman who despised her. Now here was Andy, her perfect man, her mature relationship. Except, he'd misrepresented himself.

She pressed a hand to her pounding temple. "I'm not staying here tonight."

"Nina, please."

She turned away from his aggrieved expression and scanned the room for the purse she brought with her. Spotting it on the dresser, she picked it up.

"I love you, Nina."

He wasn't playing fair.

"I love you, too," she replied, but the words didn't fall as easily from her lips as they'd done in the past.

She tucked the purse under her arm and walked out of the bedroom. Andy followed her to the front without a word. The only noise was the soft sound of their footsteps sinking into the thick carpet.

Before walking out, Nina turned to face him. He'd stopped a few feet away, hands in his pockets, worry etched in the lines across his forehead.

"How did you find out I was in New Zealand?" she asked.

He hesitated. Finally, he answered, "Gloria told me."

No surprise. Her mother thought they were a good match.

Wait a minute, that didn't make sense.

"How did you and my mother end up talking?" As far as she knew, Gloria had gotten to know the von Trapps because of her.

"Our mothers were acquaintances before you and I became friends. They struck up a friendship after going to the same spa and decided to play matchmaker. Gloria thought it would be better if I acted as if our meeting was by chance."

"Did she ask you to tell all those other lies, too?"

He winced at the harsh question. "We discussed tweaking my interests to align with yours."

"Wonderful."

With an angry spin, Nina left, not sure where she was headed, but knowing she had to get out of there.

* * *

NINA SAT in her favorite spot in the city to get ice cream, a parlor whose decor harkened back to decades earlier. The staff wore red and white uniforms, and bright posters brought attention to the daily specials. There weren't many customers at this time of night. A teen couple studied the dozens of options behind the glass, while a little boy bounced excitedly up and down in front of his mother, waiting for the clerk to finish the homemade milkshake in the noisy blender.

This booth in the window was familiar. Nina had sat here many times with her father, in this very seat. He'd sit across from her, and they'd discuss anything and everything. Whatever she wanted.

At the moment, however, she was having a conversation with her mother that she didn't want to have. Andy had called Gloria to let her know the truth was out, but in typical Gloria fashion, she showed no remorse for her behavior.

Nina sat with the phone to her ear, listening to her mother go on and on. She stared straight ahead. She didn't look left or right out the window at the people and cars passing by, too distracted by the conversation.

"Nina, honey, what he did demonstrates his love for you. Isn't that what you want?"

"And what does your role in this scenario demonstrate?" Nina asked tartly.

Gloria let out an exaggerated sigh. "This is not about me or what I did, which I don't think was that terrible, mind you. He loves you, and you fell in love with him, didn't you? So I was right to send him your way."

"I fell for a man who doesn't exist."

"On the contrary, he does exist. Everything else about him is real, but now you know he's a man willing to do anything for you. Anything to be with you. That's much more than can be said for Mr. Reese Brooks, who stomped all over your heart— your words, not mine."

"That was a long time ago," Nina muttered.

Her mother scoffed. "I'm sure he's changed since then, but not in a good way. He's gotten better at hiding his bad behavior. Trust me, I know the type. His last name might be Brooks, but he's got Johnson blood in his veins."

Nina rolled her eyes. She didn't want to hear another complaint about the Johnsons and their lack of morals or whatever other disparaging comments her mother would conjure to justify her behavior.

"I have to go. I'll talk to you later."

"Listen to me, don't make any hasty decisions. Remember how much you love this man. Don't punish Andy forever for one mistake."

"Aren't you the one who always said, when people show you who they are, believe them?"

"Yes, but of course, there are exceptions."

"Goodbye, Mom."

"Honey, he needs you. It hasn't been a year since his mother died. Remember how you felt when—"

Nina hung up and waited. When her mother didn't call back, she started eating her two scoops of ice cream, her comfort food. Tonight's flavor was caramel swirl.

When she spent the weekends with her father, he picked her up from school on Friday. After dinner, they went to get ice cream together, just the two of them. Their time to sit and chat, when she'd tell him about her fears and dreams, and he'd give her advice or simply let her talk. She missed those days. She missed her father so much right now. He'd give her advice so she'd know what to do.

She had lived with her mother, but she and her father did as much as they could together. He was her best friend. They volunteered together. They went out to dinner and the movies together. Bowling. Ice skating. He was always there, even though they had different addresses. He often invited her sister, too, but the four-year age difference meant Lindsay participated less frequently as they became older.

Her phone chirped an alert. A message from Andy.

I'm sorry. How can I fix this?

Nina: *Please stop. I need a break. Give me space.*

She didn't want to be cruel, but she needed time to think

about their situation. She turned off the ringer on the phone and turned it over so she wouldn't see his response.

"You're overdressed for this place."

The sound of his voice immediately suffused her skin with warmth, and Nina looked up into the rich brown gaze of Reese Brooks.

CHAPTER 16

*S*he could wear a plastic sack and still be overdressed for this place—any place, for that matter.

"Mind if I join you?" Reese waited, tense, for her to turn down his offer. To his surprise, she shook her head.

"Have a seat."

He set his ice cream on the table and slid into the booth.

"I'm surprised to see you here this late," she remarked.

"It's never too late for ice cream," he said, and they had a moment of understanding, which prompted smiles to both their lips.

He had been driving by when he saw her through the window and almost crashed into the car in front of him, hitting the brakes with only a few inches to spare. He parked across the street and watched her for a while, making sure she was alone as he argued with himself about whether or not he should approach. In the end, he couldn't talk himself out of spending time with her.

"I saw your mother at the domestic violence fundraiser," Nina said.

"Oh yeah? How was the event?"

He sat back and watched her, pretending to be calm when seeing her had him wired. She was such a chameleon—one minute dressed like a Bohemian in flowing dresses, peasant blouses, and a ring in her nose. The next, dressed like tonight, in a haute couture gown with spaghetti straps and a scooped neckline that hovered above her breasts, and wearing earrings that cost more than the average person's annual salary—looking like a true woman of privilege. Both looks represented her. Both looks were enough to bring him to his knees.

"Another success. When I left, the organizer confirmed they surpassed what they raised last year."

She spoke in a normal voice, but he knew Nina well enough to recognize that she wasn't herself. He'd noticed that from the street. Something was off.

"You okay?" he asked.

"Yes." She went back to eating the ice cream.

There was an awkward silence as they both ate from their containers. He hated the awkward silence and stilted sentences as they searched for the right thing to say.

Reese set down the plastic spoon. "Strange, isn't it, that we can barely find the words to talk to each other when we used to be able to talk about everything."

He had friends but he could admit he didn't experience the level of intimacy with them that he did with Nina. He wanted to know everything about her and tell her everything about himself.

She didn't have his heart. She *was* his heart.

She set down her spoon, too. "I hate it."

Her response lifted his spirits. "I hate it, too. Maybe we should fix that."

She tilted her head slightly, examining him across the table. "How?"

"Be friends again."

"You said you didn't want to be my friend."

"Yeah, well, I was blindsided by your news about…about our baby." He still had difficulty wrapping his head around what she'd divulged. She'd had years to process what happened. He still struggled with a sense of loss, the knowledge that he was almost a father and that she hadn't trusted him enough to share such a momentous part of her life with him.

Nina nodded her understanding.

"What are you doing here by yourself, anyway? Andy out of town again?" The disdain in his voice came through loud and clear, despite his best efforts.

Either she didn't notice or pretended not to. "He and I had a disagreement, and I wanted to be alone," she said in a soft voice.

Interesting.

"So, you're here, mourning over a bowl of ice cream."

"Ice cream makes everything better," she said, with a sad little smile.

"Want to talk about it?" Reese asked gently, though he didn't give a damn about Andy or their problems. As far as he was concerned, their fight was good news, but he couldn't stand seeing her hurting.

"Not really."

"What do you want to talk about?"

"Everything but that."

So that's what they did for the next forty-five minutes. She told him about her plans to roll out the volunteer program at work. He told her that he'd accepted his mother's offer to become the chief information officer at the end of the year.

She congratulated him profusely, and the more they talked, the more they relaxed, laughed, and teased each other. Being witness to her smile lit a fire inside of him and cast light in the shadows that had taken over his heart. Not for the first time, he berated his younger self, a nineteen-year-old fool who hadn't realized the jewel of a woman he had at the time.

After a while, Reese noticed the employees were covering the containers of ice cream and cleaning up behind the counter.

"Pretty soon, they're going to turn off the lights and kick us out."

Nina glanced at them moving around. She'd been as engrossed as he was in the conversation. "You're right. We better get out of here."

They tossed their containers in the trash and said goodnight to the staff. The manager let them out and locked the door behind them.

On the sidewalk, Reese stuffed his hands in his pockets as he watched the cars go up and down the dark street. "You have a ride home, or can I give you a lift?"

"A lift would be nice. Or...you could let me drive." She shot him a coy look.

"Or...you could remember that my last answer to that suggestion was 'hell no' because I don't trust you behind the wheel of my car." Reese shot her a fake smile and then looked both ways up and down the street.

"You're going to let me drive that SUV one day."

"Ha." Reese led the way across the street, and she followed behind him.

He helped her up into the vehicle and watched as she smoothed the dress over her thighs. He bit the inside of his lip to quit from groaning, wishing his hands were the ones doing the smoothing.

He slammed the door and had a stern talk with himself as he rounded the front and climbed into the driver's seat. Their easy-going banter continued on the ride to The Winthrop Hotel. Reese drove well below the speed limit to prolong their time together, and when he finally pulled up outside the hotel, disappointment replaced the levity he'd come to enjoy.

Waving away the doorman who approached to open Nina's door, he asked. "What are you up to this weekend?" He didn't want the night to end, and that was the first question he thought of to keep her in the SUV.

"Nothing major. On Saturday, I'm working with a group named Build a Home to finish construction on a house on the outskirts of town. They do the same work as Habitat for Humanity, but on a local level. We're working on a four-bedroom, three-bath house for a single dad who adopted five special-needs kids."

"What do you know about building houses?" She never ceased to amaze him with the time she put into helping others. Nina was never satisfied with simply donating money. She often physically participated in the work needed at the charities she supported.

She straightened in the seat, angling her chin higher. "I'll have you know these hands have done all kinds of work, including construction. I helped build a house in Honduras two years ago."

"Your little ass?" Reese laughed.

"Shut up!" she said, though she laughed right along with him. "Anyway, that's what I'll be up to this weekend. What do you have planned?"

He was supposed to meet a few friends in the park to play football, which seemed frivolous now and paled in comparison to the work she would be doing.

"No major plans. I could come help you guys if you need an extra pair of hands." Bonus, he'd get to spend time with Nina.

"*You?*"

"What the hell? Yeah, me."

"I'm sorry, I didn't mean to say it like that. But if you come, you have to work, Reese. It's *labor*-intensive."

He tapped his thumb on the leather steering wheel. "I'm going to ignore the insinuation that I don't know about work and point out that if President Jimmy Carter can build houses with Habitat well into his seventies, then I can build them at almost thirty, damn it. I got this. Have you forgotten I'm an athlete?"

Her eyes skimmed the muscles exposed by the short-sleeved shirt and the way his slacks fit snug on his thighs. No, she hadn't forgotten, which gave him an immense sense of satisfaction.

Nina shifted in her seat. "You can't just walk onto the site and start working. I'll make a call to the crew leader and make sure it's okay."

"Cool. Thanks."

Reese jumped out of the vehicle and opened her door. With a hand on her forearm, he helped Nina to the ground. Her skin was soft to the touch, and the fragrance she wore tonight was light—something in the rose family, for sure.

He didn't step back to give her room. She gazed up at him with vibrant brown eyes that no longer held sadness and made him want to lean in and kiss her. He stood there, way too close, with that one thought swarming in his head.

There was so much he wanted to say about how he felt and how much he'd missed her over the past five weeks, but he remained silent. A fight with her fiancé in no way meant she was ready for that conversation.

"Thanks for keeping me company," Nina said.

"No problem. Any time."

"Good night, Reese."

"Good night."

He stepped back and watched until she entered the hotel in her green satin dress. His eyes followed the swing of her hips, and he cursed quietly. She had no right to look that sexy, that elegant.

Young Nina had been quite a catch, but mature Nina was a force to be reckoned with. Andy was a damn fool. Were Reese in his shoes, he would have apologized whether or not he was wrong.

After she disappeared, he climbed into his vehicle and pulled away from the building. Coasting down the street, he stroked his jaw with one hand and considered what he'd learned.

Nina and Andy had a fight, big enough for her to go off on her own. Could there be trouble in paradise?

Man, he sure hoped so.

*　*　*

NINA UNDRESSED and climbed into bed. She rubbed the spot where Reese had held her forearm when he helped her from the Mercedes. His hold had been firm but gentle, and her skin still tingled from his touch.

As she settled under the cool cotton sheets, she looked at her phone, which she'd ignored all night. There was a message from Andy. She read it lying back against the pillows.

Andy: How long of a break do you want? One week? Two weeks?

He'd misunderstood what she meant by needing a break. She'd simply meant that she wanted to clear her head for the night, but he was suggesting a week or two of separation.

Did they need a break? Maybe time apart would be good for them. They'd been so close overseas, but now that they were back in the States, reality had struck—and so had the cold, uncomfortable truth that Andy had been deceptive. Was his deception enough to throw away their relationship after almost two years?

He wanted marriage and children. They knew many of the same people, and they cared deeply for each other. She didn't want to walk away for good yet, so a break could put their situation into better perspective.

She waited a few minutes before responding and then quickly tapped out a message before she changed her mind.

Nina: Two weeks.

The response came one minute later.

Andy: OK.

CHAPTER 17

*N*ina arrived at the Build a Home house in her low-key vehicle, a black Lexus sedan. She was still fuming with road rage after dealing with slowpokes afraid to drive over the speed limit. Then she'd flipped the bird at a guy after he cut her off, and that incident almost made her miss the exit. Honestly, people didn't know how to drive in this city, and if she didn't have Philippe to drive her around most of the time, she'd be in a perpetual state of anger every single day.

Shaking off her impatience, she walked up the driveway and greeted the familiar as well as unfamiliar faces with waves and a smile. After donning a hard hat, she walked through the house to her assigned spot. Today she'd be working on flooring, putting down carpet in two rooms and tile in the kitchen.

While new to the Build a Home family, Nina was familiar with working construction. She'd provided labor to Habitat for Humanity International on two projects during her years of travel, and the sense of accomplishment after working on a structure from the beginning until it was move-in ready was a feeling she longed to experience again.

She had volunteered several days already, so she'd come to

know some of the other volunteers well, but not so well that they knew who she was. They had no idea she was worth hundreds of millions of dollars. It was better that way, to avoid being treated differently—either by people who wanted to give her special privileges or by anyone who doubted her sincerity and tried to make her feel unwanted.

With her hair simply pulled back from her face, jeans, and no jewelry—not even her engagement ring—she looked like any other worker there, and that's exactly what she wanted.

A few minutes later, she saw Reese pull up through the window in a small two-seater, the car he drove when he didn't want to bring attention to himself. She smiled, happy he'd kept his word and shown up.

She paid him no mind and started setting up, letting Ridge, the crew leader with a red beard and mustache, meet with Reese and give him a quick overview of expectations and how they worked. Afterward, they both approached her in the living room.

As they did, she gave Reese a quick once-over. As usual, he looked unjustly amazing in a Biggie Smalls and Tupac T-shirt with jeans and boots. The outfit gave him a rugged look and caught the eyes of several of the women who angled their heads in his direction when the men walked by.

She couldn't blame them. Her hormones did a happy dance that reminded her of the first time she'd come face-to-face with him in the school parking lot after his team bludgeoned hers in a football game. She recognized him because he was an athletic star. That night, he'd been on an obvious high, with everyone vying for his attention after scoring two touchdowns, one of them after an interception catch.

But in that parking lot, he'd only had eyes for her. He blocked her path, smiled, and introduced himself, uncaring that they attended rival schools and claiming that he'd noticed her in the stands, though she couldn't fathom how that was possible among all those people.

He was the son of a billionaire. From birth, he'd received anything he wanted. That night, he wanted her, and with admirable persistence he convinced her to give up her number and go on a date. From that moment, she was lost.

Ridge pulled a pencil from behind his ear and wrote on his clipboard. "I'm going to have Reese work with you on flooring today."

"No problem," Nina said.

"If you need an extra pair of hands, grab Vivian." He turned to Reese. "Since you already know Nina, I'll leave you two alone. I'm sure you know she'll take good care of you." Ridge went outside to speak to an older guy using an electric saw to cut wood in the yard.

"You're not going to be a slave driver, are you?" Reese asked, his low voice sounding more like a man in the middle of a seduction instead of someone having a conversation about laying flooring.

From beneath the hard hat, he looked down at her with lowered eyelids, as if he was about to go to sleep. But it wasn't a sleepy look. He was almost...predatory, his gaze skating over her bare fingers before traveling over her hips and breasts.

"Only if you deserve it," Nina said.

"And of course, you're the person who determines if I deserve it or not."

"Exactly. I'm going to have fun bossing you around."

Reese groaned, which sounded much more sexual than she'd expected because it reminded her of the night he'd kissed her. He'd groaned like that when he pressed his face between her legs.

Her skin flushed hot, and she refocused on the words coming out of his mouth.

"I hope I didn't make a mistake coming here," Reese said.

"You didn't. Come on, let me show you what to do." She pointed out their tools and explained the process of installing carpet. When she finished, she rested her hands on her hips. "Got it?"

"Got it," Reese confirmed.

They went to work, first installing the tack strips around the room and then putting down the carpet padding. They worked well together, and he was a fast learner and good at following directions. At various stages in the process, he wore an adorable frown of concentration, a carbon copy of the one he wore when working on a computer problem.

Halfway through the morning shift, they took a break with the rest of the workers. Nina hung back at the door while Reese chatted up a few of the guys outside. He fit right in, but she'd never doubted he would. Reese had charisma and a friendly personality, so it was hard not to like him.

"Who is that?" The voice behind her left ear belonged to Vivian, someone she'd become friends with since the first day on site.

"Who?" Nina asked, feigning ignorance.

Vivian, who wore her hair in a bleached-blonde short natural, came to stand beside her. She folded her arms. "Your friend. He's hot." Vivian knew about Andy, so it was no surprise she didn't assume Reese and Nina were a couple.

"You're not here to pick up men." Nina kept her voice light, though irritated by Vivian's comment.

"Says who?" Vivian's voice went lower. "My uncle advised me that if I wanted to meet men outside of the usual work and club environment, I should do volunteer work. I'd get in some hours as a good citizen, and a side perk is that I might meet a nice man." She winked after dropping that gem of knowledge.

"You should probably set your sights elsewhere," Nina said.

"He's too fine to pass up. I'm going to introduce myself."

"You're going to be disappointed. He's already taken," Nina

said. She didn't know why she lied. She wasn't protecting Reese because, aside from being a bit chatty at times, Vivian was a great person.

Vivian's face fell. "Of course he is. All of the fine ones are." Her face brightened. "You know what, I didn't see a ring on his finger, and I don't see his woman here with him. As far as I'm concerned, I still have a chance."

Before Nina could discourage her, Vivian sashayed her way over to where the men stood and introduced herself to Reese.

A nasty emotion claimed Nina, and though she didn't want to give a name to it, she knew exactly what it was. Jealousy.

Watching from a distance, she reached to twist the ring on her finger—a habit she'd developed ever since she accepted Andy's proposal—and was met with the stark emptiness of her finger. She swallowed back the ugly green monster that threatened to choke her as she listened to Reese's laughter—a hearty and robust sound that matched the pure joy on his face.

He fit so well into any situation, and she wondered if Andy would have been as comfortable here. Overseas, she'd always taken the lead in making friends and learning more about the people they met on their journey. She never judged him for it because not everyone had an outgoing personality. Some people were quieter than others, but today certainly made her aware of the contrasting personalities between both men.

Her attention lingered on Reese, and when his eyes swept the area and found hers, emotion stomped through her chest, and her eyes and nose burned with tears that came out of nowhere. She couldn't go down this road with him again.

She gave him a quick smile, spun away from the door, and went inside to compose herself.

When the break ended, Reese joined her in the dining room where they'd left off.

"Everything okay?" he asked.

"Uh-huh. Everything is fine." At least, now that she'd regained her composure. "Ready to get back to work?"

"Let's do this." He rubbed his palms together.

This time around, her awareness of him increased exponentially. She couldn't help but notice the beauty of his hands as he secured the carpet at the seams. When he asked a question, his voice was more attractive and his laugh more appealing. She stepped back and let him use the carpet stretcher, and he worked deftly, muscles bunching and elongating with each movement, captivating her attention and making her fidgety.

She was relieved when Ridge alerted them that lunchtime was near. She needed the break from the thoughts of Reese kissing all over her body, or his face pressed between her legs. Those lewd thoughts resulted in aching breasts and unwanted wetness between her thighs.

Swallowing hard, she guiltily pushed the fantasies away, but they persevered like ocean waves that continuously rolled back onto the shore.

CHAPTER 18

$\mathcal{W}$aving his hands overhead, Ridge caught everyone's attention before they left the site for lunch. Nina, Reese, and the rest of the workers created a semi-circle around him outside of the house to hear his announcement.

"We have a nice surprise today. An anonymous donor is treating us all to lunch."

Gasps and cheers went up from the group.

"Where from?" a male voice asked from the back.

"Ivy's Restaurant, you lucky slobs. Today we're eating like royalty."

Whoops of joy filled the yard, and Vivian turned wide eyes to Nina. "I've always wanted to eat there. Yes!"

"Aren't we lucky," Nina said to Reese.

"Aren't we, though?" Except for a faint smile that played around his lips, his face remained expressionless.

"And here they are!" Ridge announced.

More cheers filled the air when two unmarked white vans pulled up to the curb.

Four workers, two from each van, hopped out and introduced themselves and then went to work setting up in the backyard where there was more shade and the temperature cooler.

The ones from the second van set up tables and chairs with help from some of the volunteers. More volunteers helped the two from the first van set up tables where they placed chafing dishes filled with the entree options. There was plenty of food for their twenty-person group, and everything looked and smelled divine. The entree options were roasted chicken garnished with strips of pearl onions, lemon-baked fish, and a vegetarian option with sautéed vegetables. Sides included potato puree, rice pilaf, red and gold beets in a sweet vinaigrette, spinach salad, and crusty bread.

The servers spooned generous servings onto each plate, adding additional helpings for anyone who requested extra portions. Reese sat down across from two of the men he'd been talking to earlier, and when Nina saw Vivian making a beeline for the empty chair next to him, she quickly plopped down in the unoccupied space and pretended not to notice Vivian's pout as she turned away.

"You want something to drink?" Reese asked when he saw she didn't have a beverage.

"That would be nice. Water, please," Nina said.

He was such a gentleman. Another mark in his column. Not that she kept score.

He got her a bottle of water and reclaimed his seat.

"How long have you been volunteering for Build a Home?" one of the men asked Reese.

If memory served her correctly, the man's name was Dean. He'd worked construction for years and after retirement, started volunteering in the program.

"This is my first time," Reese answered. He sliced into a chicken breast.

"No shit. This isn't my first day, but it's my first project," said the man next to Dean, a retired teacher with dark hair.

"I'm here because my wife wanted me out of her hair. Ended up liking the work, so I volunteer for Habitat and these guys," Dean said, with a laugh.

"You must really enjoy doing this work to volunteer with both organizations," Nina said.

"On a day like today, with all this good food, I love it," Dean replied.

They all laughed.

"I like it, too," Reese said.

"So you'll volunteer for Build a Home again?' Nina asked.

"I would."

"One thing I've learned in the few days I've been doing this," the teacher started, "is that there's a helluva lot of satisfaction that comes from helping someone else, you know what I mean?"

Nina, Reese, and Dean nodded.

Nina stabbed a gold beet with her fork, but before she put it in her mouth, said, "I've done a lot of volunteer work over the years. It's something my father instilled in me. The funny thing is, I'm supposed to be helping people, but there have been times when I feel like I get more out of the experience than they do. Does that make sense?"

Dean nodded his agreement. "I completely understand. I can't say I always come back for selfless reasons. The shit feels good." He glanced at Nina. "Pardon my French."

She smiled to let him know the curse didn't bother her.

"Feels real good, and the company's not so bad, either." Reese slid a glance at Nina.

The four of them lapsed into other topics, and before long, their thirty-minute lunch break turned into forty-five minutes, at which point Ridge reminded everyone they had more work to do to complete the house.

With groans, full bellies, and words of thanks to the Ivy's

Restaurant staff, the workers lumbered back to their tasks with a little less enthusiasm than before.

* * *

THE DAY ENDED on a high note. They finished the house, and at the end, Ridge asked everyone to stand in the front yard. He set up a camera and hustled over to where the group stood and slid into the photo with them.

Before they all dispersed, Vivian came over to Reese.

"It was really nice to meet you. Hopefully, I'll see you on another project in the future." She extended her hand.

"Maybe you will," he said.

He shook her hand, and she pressed a slip of paper against his palm. He should have been expecting that because she had not been shy about letting him know she was interested.

With a wink, she walked away toward her vehicle.

Nina approached, and Reese stuck his hand into his pocket. "I'll walk you to your car. Did you drive?" he asked.

"Yes."

"Oh, shit."

"Funny." She glared at him. "Are you going to call her?" she asked, taking off toward her car.

Of course she saw. "No." Reese walked behind her, his gaze dropping to the way the tight jeans lovingly squeezed her behind.

"Why not?"

"Not interested."

They stopped at her Lexus, parked under the shade of a tree, and he placed a hand on the rooftop.

"She'll be disappointed."

If he didn't know better, he'd say Nina was jealous.

"Won't be the first time I disappointed a woman," he said with meaning.

She averted her eyes and scuffed the toe of her shoe against the pavement. "So, you enjoyed yourself?" Her voice sounded a little anxious, as if his reply was very important to her.

"Yeah, like I said at lunch, this was a good experience. Now I understand your passion for the work you do."

Helping out also reminded him of a tenet his maternal grandfather had instilled in his children. He believed they were in a unique position to leave the world in a better state than they found it, and it was their moral obligation to do so.

His grandfather had mostly been concerned with giving large donations to nonprofit organizations and attending charity functions. Today made Reese appreciate the act of engaging instead of only throwing money at an issue. He saw where both could fit into his life.

"Nice of you to feed us."

"I had nothing to do with that. An anonymous donor fed us, remember?"

"Sure." She smiled at him. "A friend and I are going to the movies later, so I better get out of here if I don't want to be late."

Going out, but not with Andy. Were they still mad at each other? He wanted to ask but decided not to.

"Okay, I won't keep you, but if you're looking for something to get into tomorrow night, you should come by Club Masquerade. They're having a ladies' night where they only play songs by female artists. I'll be in the VIP and can leave your name at the door."

His brother-in-law, Cameron, owned Club Masquerade with his siblings. It was the hottest night club in Atlanta and often had themed nights to encourage people to come out.

"Um, sounds tempting, but since it's Sunday night and I'm going to the office on Monday morning, I don't think I'll be able to make it."

"I'll place your name on the list anyway, and if you don't come, we can hang out another time."

"That sounds good. I better get going. See you later."

She entered her car, and he stepped back so she could drive off.

Reese slowly walked to his vehicle, waving at Dean, who pulled away in his truck. When he stuck his hands in his pocket to fish out the keys, he encountered the scrap of paper Vivian had written her number on.

In the past, he would have kept those digits and invited her to the VIP tomorrow night. But right now, he had no interest in meaningless hookups. Not when for the second time he'd seen Nina in three days she wasn't wearing her ring, *and* not once had she mentioned plans with Andy.

He crumbled the number, jogged over to the dumpster, and tossed it in. Then he climbed into his car and drove off.

Today made him reevaluate his life and want to do more, which made him think about his sister, Simone. As the philanthropic ambassador for the Johnson Foundation, she promoted the organization and its causes. She'd temporarily slowed down her work since having a baby last October, but if anyone could point him in the right direction, she could.

He dialed his sister's number over the Bluetooth.

After three rings, Simone's groggy voice came on the line. "Hello?"

"Did I wake you?" he asked.

She yawned. "I dozed off. Cameron went to the club early, and me and the little guy fell asleep on the sofa. What's up?"

Reese turned on his indicator and switched lanes. "I'm wondering how I can help the Johnson Foundation, but I'm not interested in only attending fundraisers. I want to be hands-on."

"Oh." She sounded understandably surprised. "What do you want to do?"

"I don't know. Do you have a list?"

"I can put one together and send it over."

"That sounds good. Thanks."

"What brought this on?"

"I worked with Build a Home today with Nina." Reese slowed to a stop at a red light.

"What's that?"

"They're like Habitat for Humanity, but on a much smaller scale. It might be an organization the foundation could support."

"So, it's a charitable organization?"

"Yes."

"And you went there because…?"

"Nina invited me, and I helped complete construction on a house today."

"I see," she said, her voice heavy with meaning.

"Don't start."

She laughed. "Okay. Were you interested in any specific kind of work?"

"Projects where I can get my hands dirty. I liked the physical aspect of today's job, but I'm not limited to that."

"Most of my projects are with kids, but around the holidays, we need help at the food banks. We also need more help with the men's coat closet project. You could sort through donations and help men in the store put together outfits. Oh! I just thought of something. We're funding computer labs in several of the YMCAs around the city. You could volunteer at the centers if you're interested."

"I'm interested in all of that."

"You won't have time to do everything, but I'll put together options with the information about what kind of help is needed where."

"Perfect." Reese pulled off when the light turned green.

"What's Nina's mailing address? I need to send her a thank-you card." Amusement filled Simone's voice.

"If you do that, I'll never forgive you."

She giggled. "I appreciate your interest. Bye. Love you."

"Love you, too."

Reese barely registered the ride to his apartment. Now that he'd communicated his interest to his sister, all he could think about was Nina. She said she wouldn't come tomorrow night, but he hoped she changed her mind.

CHAPTER 19

$\mathcal{H}$e should have stayed home.

Restless, Reese stood up in the White Room on the mezzanine level of Club Masquerade and thrust aside the white curtains to go onto the balcony and look down at the gyrating bodies dancing to the "Ladies' Night" remix by Lil' Kim. Strobe lights crisscrossed the ceiling and added to the party atmosphere on an unusually packed Sunday night.

He knew almost everyone in the VIP but didn't want to party with them. He was in a crabby mood. What the hell was wrong with him? He used to enjoy this shit.

Partying. Drinking. Screwing around. Activities that all seemed so...pointless now. He knew why but didn't want to admit the reason. Didn't want to think about *Nina*.

He swirled a snifter of brandy and lifted the tapered mouth of the glass to his lips, taking a sip. He needed to get out of there. It didn't make sense to stay if he wasn't having a good time. He could be at home, coding software, or tinkering with one of his computer projects. Anything would be better than being here, waiting for her to show up and knowing she wouldn't.

He drained what was left in the glass and then slipped behind the curtain. He was about to say good night to the nine other people who'd occupied the white couches and chairs with him when the air became trapped in his lungs.

Nina stood on the edge of the room, obviously searching for him. Thank goodness he hadn't left. When she saw him, her eyes lit up, and his restlessness, anxiety, and upset faded away with her smile.

Though she had a great figure, Nina didn't always wear figure-hugging clothes. She caught the eye because she radiated light, and tonight she looked exquisite in a loose-fitting mustard-yellow dress that was completely wrong for this venue —where so many women showed cleavage or wore tight and short outfits—but was absolutely right for her.

The flowy hemline of the halter-topped dress hid her ankles but allowed a peek at gold, open-toed sandals. Her jewelry consisted of a gold stud in her nose, gold earrings, and two gold cuffs that circled her upper right arm. No engagement ring, though.

Adding to her allure, she styled her thick hair in a neat twist-out that brushed her shoulders and framed her face. She was a goddess. No, that was too tame of a word. She looked other-worldly, ethereal.

Affecting nonchalance, Reese set down the empty glass and strolled over to where she stood. "I thought you weren't coming."

She smelled good enough to eat, and if they weren't in a public place, he might have dropped to his knees, spread her legs wide, and eaten his fill.

"I wasn't, but then I changed my mind. I hope I'm not too late." She looked around the room.

"You're right on time." He gathered her up in his arms, squeezing her tight and hating that he'd have to release her. He wanted to hold her hostage the way she'd held his heart hostage all these years.

He kissed her soft cheek, and her hair brushed his face. With regret, he set her back on her feet, and she laughed breathlessly, smoothing a hand along her hairline.

"What was that for?" she asked.

"That was for me."

Reese ignored the question in her eyes and with a hand at her waist, introduced her to the group, but she knew most everyone there because they knew a lot of the same people.

At the end of the introductions, he took Nina by the hand and asked a guy on the white loveseat to let them sit there. The guy immediately vacated the spot, and Reese pulled her onto the loveseat beside him, so close their thighs touched.

When she sat, the dress shifted and exposed her smooth left thigh. Damn. There was a long split in the dress. She was trying to kill him. Sexual hunger ground through his gut with a vengeance.

He stretched an arm across the back of the chair and leaned in under the pretense of needing to be heard above the music. "I'm glad you came."

Nina looked at him from beneath lowered lashes. "Me, too. I needed to get out of the house."

"How was the movie with your friend yesterday?"

"Good. I hadn't seen her since I came back. We went to dinner afterward and had fun catching up."

"Where's your ring?"

"At home."

"Where's your man?"

She lowered her gaze. "I'd rather not talk about him right now. I just want to have fun tonight."

His forefinger made slow circles on the back of her neck, and her body tensed, but she didn't move away. He considered that a good sign.

"We can definitely have fun tonight," he promised.

They spent time together, whispering and having the occasional cocktail, but they also spent time talking to their friends.

As more invitees showed up and brought guests with them, the VIP filled up. Pretty soon, the White Room became packed, with half of the group dancing and the other half mingling and enjoying the food that kept coming in a steady flow from the kitchen.

A couple of romantic connections occurred throughout the night. His friend Mark danced with a woman who'd arrived as a guest of her sister. A guy he didn't know had slipped away with the sister, and he had no idea where they'd gone off to.

As always, his eyes came back to Nina. Holding a chocolate martini, she swayed to the music while in conversation with two other women. Something was wrong with her and Andy. Had they split up? They must have. Otherwise, why wouldn't she be wearing her ring, again? Oddly enough, she didn't seem heartbroken. She looked happy and at ease and very, very single.

The guitar opening of Ashanti's "Only You" started, and Nina and the two women let out squeals and raised their glasses. Hands in the air, they danced to the music, tossing their hips left to right in time to the beat.

When she caught him watching, she excused herself and came over to where he stood at a bistro table.

"Come dance with me," she said, setting down her glass.

"No, you go ahead."

"Come on. Please." She stuck out her lower lip.

Reese laughed. "That's not going to work. You know I don't dance."

"You danced at Lindsay's wedding reception."

"An exception, remember? It was just a little two-step."

"Fine." Nina shimmied back over to where her two friends were dancing with each other. The three of them formed a circle and moved to the music, and he was content to simply watch her.

The song ended, and another Ashanti tune, "Focus," started. The roar that went up from the group echoed on the main dance floor of the club below. More people jumped up and created a mass of twirling and shaking bodies.

The DJ did a heck of a job keeping the club-goers hyped. The place crackled with energy, and Reese sensed a shift in the air. One that made him hyperaware of his surroundings, and hyperaware of the woman who'd snagged his attention since she arrived like a ray of sunshine in yellow and gold.

As he watched, one of his male friends danced up behind Nina. Bishop, someone he'd become friends with in recent years. He didn't know Nina or that she and Reese used to date, which made her off-limits.

Bishop tapped Nina's shoulder and startled, she glanced back at him. She smiled and said, "Hi."

Reese couldn't hear her but read her lips. His eyes zeroed in on her swaying hips and the way she looked back at Bishop. She smiled seductively and then did something unexpected. She shot a quick glance at Reese, their gazes binding together before she looked away.

Her expression warmed his gut before the sensation crawled lower and made his dick raise its head. He didn't think he'd read the message in her eyes wrong. She was dancing *with* Bishop but dancing *for* Reese.

He strolled over and tapped Bishop on the shoulder. When he looked back, Reese jerked his thumb, a clear indication he needed to leave. "That's me," he said.

"What?" Bishop said irritably.

Apparently, he wanted his ass kicked from one end of the VIP to the other.

Reese stepped closer so they were almost nose to nose. "That's me."

Bishop threw up his hands, not wanting any trouble. "All right. Damn."

Reese slid into the space he vacated and placed his hands on Nina's hips. She still hadn't turned around yet. His blood heated when she bent her knees and dropped a little lower. His grip tightened, and he pulled her back against him.

She looked at him from the corner of her eye but didn't flinch or act surprised that he was behind her instead of Bishop. She'd either seen him approach or had expected him to come for her.

His hands skated up her sides as she moved in a snakelike manner to the music, and he bent his head to her neck, one arm hugging her torso from behind while his hand encircled her delicate throat. He pressed his body to hers, swiveling his hips to match her movements. Her back lay flush against his chest, and her full bottom fit snug against his erection because he didn't let her move away from him. She made each of her movements with him glued to her like they were one and couldn't budge an inch without him right there, grinding against her to the bass beat.

They danced like that for the next song as well, and he endured the torture because he was finally holding her in his arms the way he'd longed to do.

When the music slowed to "It Kills Me" by Melanie Fiona, people sauntered off the dance floor, but not them. Reese turned Nina to face him and folded his arms across her shoulders. Now they faced each other, and all her softness smashed into him—thighs, stomach, breasts. As the song crescendoed to the chorus, he dropped his head close to hers. Her breathing accelerated, her sweet breath blowing against his mouth with each pant.

He kept his head bent over her and gently rubbed his lips against the shell of her ear and the tender spot on the side of her neck.

Her hands slipped under his shirt in a wanton display of her need to touch him. They were barely dancing now, mostly grinding. This was merely foreplay as they rocked to the music, and as their hands explored each other's bodies, their caresses became bolder, edging toward the obscene.

His hand climbed higher to her neck, and using his thumb, he tilted her head up to him. Her closed eyes fluttered open, exposing the red-hot arousal in their depths.

Nina raised up on tiptoe to kiss him, but he lifted his head out of reach to take a good look at her.

Her eyes filled with confusion. She was so horny, rubbing her whole body up against him. Her thighs slid against his, and one foot slipped up and down his calf. Her panties had to be soaked. He was definitely fucking her tonight.

"You're killing me, you know that?" Reese said in a low voice.

He brushed her lips with his, and when she didn't reject him, he claimed her mouth outright, right in the middle of the floor for everyone to see.

Reese plucked her lower lip between his. The teasing forced her to tighten her arms around his waist and press closer. He kissed the corner of her mouth, and her eyes fluttered closed.

He massaged the back of her neck, gently squeezing and letting go, prepping her, getting her hot and ready to give him what should have been his all along.

Grabbing a fistful of her soft hair, Reese pressed his mouth hard to hers. No tongue. Just their lips tight against each other.

He wanted her, and she wanted him. The tension stacked between them had reached an almost unbearable level, resulting in the painful effects of pounding hunger in his loins.

"Let's get out of here," Reese said.

Without another word to anyone, he took her by the hand and led the way.

CHAPTER 20

*R*eese tapped his thumb impatiently on the steering wheel.

The traffic was horrendous. There must be an accident somewhere up the street. Atlanta traffic could be a nightmare any time of the day or day of the week, but right now had to be the worst time in history for there to be a long line of cars inching along at a sloth's pace.

"*Fuuuck!*" He slammed his hand against the wheel and craned his neck in vain to find the problem. Not that it mattered. If he saw what caused the traffic jam, he couldn't do anything about it.

"Reese, pull over."

Nina spoke in a calm voice, but she appeared to be anything but calm. Instead, as anxious as he was, with turbulent emotion flaring in her eyes.

"Pull over," she said again, softer this time. She placed a hand on his thigh, and his muscles tensed. With that single touch, she generated enough heat to start a forest fire.

Nothing else needed to be said. The out-of-control desire that consumed him consumed her, too.

The minute Reese saw an opening, he made a sharp right down a side street, away from the crawling traffic, and parked in the shadows.

The honking horns became a distant sound compared to the quiet in the car. Reese turned to Nina and held her chin, tilting her face up to his. Her full lips parted as her chest heaved up and down, and he swooped his mouth down on hers in an open-mouthed kiss. His tongue delved between her lips, tasting the sweet nectar of her mouth, and she shivered. She tasted like heaven. Better than the finest chocolate, her flavor bursting on his tongue and making him dizzy with the need and hunger that filled every part of him.

The anniversary night of her father's death came back with a vengeance. The control he'd had to exercise so as not to take advantage of her emotional state was no longer a factor. He unsnapped her seatbelt and pulled her closer, threading his fingers into her thick, kinky hair.

He explored the velvety softness of her lips, but as much as he enjoyed the mouth-to-mouth contact, the position was awkward. Reese lifted his head.

"This isn't going to work."

"Yes, it is," she insisted, leaning in and fastening her mouth to his again.

She was so eager. So greedy. Reese groaned and held her head, kissing her thoroughly with a loud, wet kiss.

But he lifted his head again and gazed down into her sex-hungry eyes. "Let's get in the back seat. It's better."

With the awkward twisting and shifting of his long body, Reese climbed into the back. Nina removed her shoes, and he helped her do the same, his arms and hands serving to help keep her balance.

Giggling, she settled on his lap and straddled his thighs.

Reese brushed her hair back from her face. "What's so funny?"

"We haven't gotten any better at climbing into the back seat. Remember that night at the park when we almost got caught in your car?"

He'd forgotten about that time. He planned to have her spend the night in his room, but his mother came back early from a business trip, and they'd had to make do at the park. When a police car cruised into the area, they'd scrambled to put on the few items of clothing they'd removed.

"I remember that. You were scared," he said softly, smiling into her eyes.

"And you weren't. Meanwhile, I was terrified we'd get caught, and my father would be so disappointed in me."

Reese grinned. "I corrupted you."

"You did," she said softly, edging her face closer.

"Still worried about getting caught?" Reese asked, searching her eyes.

"Not tonight."

Reese took her mouth in another deep kiss. He wanted her horizontal, but this would have to do.

Sweeping her hair to the side, he kissed the curve of her throat and felt her pulse beat against the tip of his tongue. He tasted the delicate line of her jaw and kissed the shell of her ear. Her breathy moans encouraged him as he pushed his hands up under her dress and spread them over her velvety thighs. Sliding his hands higher, he encountered string and lace.

He was so excited, if he didn't calm down, he'd prematurely nut in his pants. He needed her so badly that he almost didn't care about such an embarrassing spectacle. He'd simply make it up to her during the next round.

He unfastened her top and dragged it down to reveal her full, heavy breasts. Burying his face in the scented valley they created, he squeezed them together and then smoothed his hand up and down her arched back, listening to her moan his name. Lifting one breast into his mouth, he tugged on the walnut-colored nipple with his teeth and lips until it puckered into a tight little stone. Her fingernails gently scraped his scalp as she massaged his crown and bowed her back to force her nipple deeper into his mouth.

"Reese...*Reese.*"

His name was a litany of praise on her lips. As he feasted on her breasts, his hands smoothed up and down her arched spine. He squeezed her ass and grabbed her thighs, inflamed by her sounds of pleasure and the sensual way she moved.

He wasn't the only one doing the touching. She touched him, too. She kissed him and sucked his tongue into her mouth while her hands traversed the muscles of his back and shoulders. She rubbed her body against him, grinding her hips into his until he was panting and gripping her dress in a desperate fight to keep from letting go.

Nina unbuttoned his shirt, letting her tongue taste his chest, circle his nipples, and trail across his pecs. When she reached down and massaged his length, his head fell back as a groan burst from his throat. Having her hands on him was better than a dream come true, and his thighs hardened as he reveled in her touch.

"Nina." He grabbed a handful of hair and gave her a bruising kiss that caused her to whimper into his mouth but kiss him back just as hard.

His fingers found her wet clit and massaged until she writhed against his digits. When he could tell she was near to climax, he jerked away his hand, and she made a loud, impatient sound and gripped his shirt. She buried her face in his neck so he couldn't read her expression.

"Reese, *please.*"

"I got you," he whispered in her ear.

This would be a true quickie because the temperature in the car had already reached scalding. He lifted up and pulled out his wallet, and after removing a condom, tossed it to the seat.

"Hurry," she begged. "Please, Reese."

His hands shook from the urgency in her voice and the cramped quarters of the car. He slipped on the protection and with two hard yanks, broke the strings on either side of her thong. Nina gasped, her eyes going wide as he tossed the torn fabric to the floor.

"Get on this dick."

She lifted onto her knees and with his hands guiding her hips, sank onto his throbbing length.

They both froze, breathing suspended at the magnitude of this moment and their oneness, after so very long. When her head fell back on a sharp cry, the sound of raw, naked pleasure had him grabbing her ass and gritting his teeth.

The tight clasp of her body around him was unlike anything he'd ever experienced. This was nirvana, the greatest pleasure he'd ever know. He was deep in the woman he adored, the woman that he loved. Loved so much that at times he believed that his feelings were deeper than love.

Reese prayed he didn't come too fast because he wanted to make her feel good and have this moment be as enjoyable as possible for both of them. Grabbing the globes of her soft bottom, he pumped into her hard, desperately. As if he'd never get another chance to be with her like this again. Everything could change in the morning. But this...this he could relive over and over, long after the night came to an end.

Fuck Saint Andy. Fuck everybody. Tonight, Nina was his. This was where she belonged—riding *his* dick. Moaning *his* name. She was *his* woman. He was claiming her.

He sank his teeth into her neck like a lion would its prey. Then he soothed the bite with his moist tongue.

Reese leaned back, swinging his hips upward, driving his hard body into hers. With her arms draped over his shoulders and her head thrown back, she bounced up and down and sent her breathless pants to the ceiling of the car. The fullness of her jostling breasts mesmerized him. They crashed against each other, and the dark nipples hypnotized him with their left-to-right motion. Reese groaned and shut his eyes, welcoming the darkness for a few seconds, or he'd come too fast, but the sounds of her husky cries and the scent of perfume and sex that filled the car almost made him come anyway.

One hand on her waist, the other gripping her bottom under the dress, Reese spread his legs wider and added more leverage to each thrust. The vehicle rocked under the strain of their frantic coupling, and he knew if they got caught now he'd never be able to stop. He was too far gone, loving the sensation of her wet heat stretched around his hard flesh as he drowned in her juices.

The pitch of her cries went higher, and he knew she was close. He watched with fascination as she caressed her own stomach and fondled her own breasts. Shit, she was so damn sexy. Then with two solid strokes and his whispered, "Come for me baby," she climaxed with a keening cry that filled the car and made the skin on the back of his neck tingle.

Her fingers tightened on her breasts to intensify the orgasm. Reese licked one nipple exposed between her parted fingers and then came hard with a guttural groan that tore from his throat. He buried his face in her neck and clutched her tight, gasping. Nina clung to him, too, moaning her satisfaction as her body trembled through the aftershock.

In the back seat of his Mercedes, their sweat-damp bodies were nothing but a bundle of tight, clinging limbs.

This was it. She was it for him.

Reese looped an arm around her neck and kissed her jawline. "Nina." He breathed her name like a prayer and sighed into her neck—this mature, independent, carefree, adventurous woman with a big heart.

As he held her close, inhaling the sweet scent of her neck, he knew no other woman would do. Nina touched his heart, his soul, his mind, his body. His head emptied of everything but her. Her touch, the way she smelled. She simply consumed him and all of his senses.

After a long while, they eased apart, and her eyes held that sleepy, hazy look that came from fantastic sex. That expression hadn't changed in all these years. It was still such a beautiful sight.

He gently kissed her mouth and then lavished the same affection on each of her breasts. He fondled their lushness until her hot little butt squirmed against him in a needy way.

"I want to lay you in a bed and make love to you properly. You deserve more than a quick screw in the back of my car. I want to see all of you. I want to touch you everywhere and take my time kissing every inch of you. Let me take you home. Tell me you want that, too."

Nina nodded.

He looked into her eyes. "Say it."

"I do." Her husky voice trembled a little. "I want to make love to you all night. I want to feel like this over and over—"

He interrupted her sentence with a frantic kiss that fused their mouths together. The beast had been unleashed.

Their night had just begun.

CHAPTER 21

*T*hey disrobed inside the door of her apartment.

Nina dropped her dress, and Reese removed his shirt to reveal sculpted muscle under smooth, fawn-colored skin.

They left the pile of clothes behind as he climbed the stairs in the dark with her wrapped around him. In the bedroom, he laid her on the bed and hovered over her on his elbows. As his gaze traveled up and down her body, she melted under the affection and desire displayed in his eyes.

"Damn, you're so beautiful, Nina," he whispered. His intoxicating words filled her with warmth.

She placed a hand at the back of his head and pulled his face closer. "You, too," she whispered.

Their lovemaking was gentler than before, their caresses slow and unhurried. He touched her everywhere like he said he would, leaving no part of her body unexplored. His hands smoothed down her belly and over her thighs and knees. Wherever they went, his mouth followed in a thorough review that left her trembling and downright begging for his possession.

Her aching body squirmed in delirium as his tongue

wreaked havoc between her thighs by drawing lazy circles around her clit while he sucked her lower lips with masterful precision. Tilting her head back, she whispered his name, losing herself in a connection that touched not only her body but somewhere deep in her heart.

She floated on a cloudy haze of passion administered by the only man who'd ever made her feel this way. The kisses on her neck and face were affectionate yet arousing. His hands on her hips and breasts brought pleasure and familiar comfort.

"Reese." His name was a moan on her lips, whispered over and over like an incantation. She couldn't seem to stop saying his name. How many times had she whispered or moaned it in the past hour? She wanted him so much, right in the center where she ached the most. "Take me, please."

Reese slipped a condom over his hard length. "Say it again."

"Please, Reese. Take—"

He thrust into her slick entrance. Lifting her knees into the groove of his elbows, he kept her under control, at the mercy of each of his pleasure-inducing thrusts.

"You never have to beg for this dick," he rasped. He maintained a steady rhythm of advance and retreat. "It's yours whenever you want it."

His body moved inside hers with slow deliberation, laboring over her with long, sturdy pumps of his hips. She was a slave to his rhythm, barely able to move with her legs pinned against her breasts.

Reese kept hitting her spot in an effort to coax the orgasm to come out of hiding. Kissing her passionately, with their tongues and teeth and lips tangling in disarray, and not once did he ever break stride.

"I know you don't have this with him. You're mine, Nina. You're *mine.*"

Like a stopper yanked from a bottle, his words discharged her orgasm, and she exploded around him with soft little cries.

Reese sucked in a sharp breath and kept driving into her as she rode out the storm of tremors.

It was too much. Sex with him was too much. Panting, Nina shut her eyes and shuddered as Reese kissed her neck and propelled himself deeper and harder as he came, too.

Overwhelmed and feeling out of control, she turned her head and let the pillow grab the cries that broke from her throat and capture the tears of sheer joy that squeezed from between her tightly closed eyelids.

* * *

REESE HAD AN INSATIABLE APPETITE. Exhausted, Nina finally pleaded for a break, and he gave her one. He lay wrapped around her from behind as thunder rolled across the sky like giant boulders, and the soothing music of raindrops hit the windows continuously.

"Your hair smells different." His voice was husky and low because they'd dozed off for a couple of hours and woken up when the sound of the storm penetrated their shallow sleep. Dawn would soon come.

"You like it?"

He buried his face in her hair and sniffed. "Yeah. Smells like ginger and something else I can't quite place."

"That's probably the coconut. I'm using a new plant-based product line that's supposed to add more moisture to my hair."

He twirled some of her hair around his fingers. "I believe it. Your curls were really defined."

"Were?"

"Well, they've fallen quite a bit," he said, sounding amused and smug.

Nina could only imagine what her hair looked like now. "I can't believe you noticed the difference in my hair."

"I notice everything about you."

They lapsed into silence and listened to the storm outside, but her mind stayed busy. His ability to make her feel special was what made Reese so dangerous. He did so with words but also with actions.

He had a ready smile for everyone, especially her. His eyes lit up whenever he saw her, which was one of the reasons she'd fallen so hard for him back in the day. It was impossible not to fall for someone who behaved as if the very sight of you brightened their day the way the sun did when it took its place in the sky every morning.

Reese became unusually still. "I have a question for you."

"Okay," Nina said cautiously.

"Did...did losing our baby hurt?" He sounded hesitant, as if unsure if that was an appropriate question.

The memory of her suffering had dimmed significantly over the years but hadn't completely disappeared. Yet that experience paled in comparison to the emotional trauma of losing their baby after eighteen weeks. She still recalled the sense of defeat she'd experienced. She'd failed in her relationship and failed at having a baby. A baby she'd wanted desperately after her initial fears had been dealt with.

Nina answered his question truthfully. "Yes, losing our baby was very painful, and there was a lot of blood, but the emotional pain stayed with me longer than the physical pain. I never got to hold him. I never got to see his face."

Reese's thumb gently stroked across the back of her hand. "Were you alone?"

"My mother and Lindsay came to the hospital with me. My dad flew back from overseas when he found out." Her mother had never cared for Reese because of her personal prejudice against his mother's family, but the miscarriage marked the day her father no longer had a kind word to say about Reese.

It didn't matter that Reese didn't know about the baby. As far as

Tyrus was concerned, Reese had brought her nothing but pain. Their closeness meant he'd seen her cry over the breakup, and then he had a front-row seat to her suffering because Reese had gotten her pregnant. He strongly advised her to stay away from him, but she'd only managed to do that for a little over a year. Reese wore her down, but the truth was, she had missed him all along.

"I would have been there for you, too. I would have held your hand or done whatever you needed me to do. I wish you'd told me."

"I wish I'd told you, too." Her voice was thick with sorrow.

Reese kissed her right shoulder blade and tightened his arms around her. She regretted letting her feelings get in the way of sharing such an important event with him. Looking back, she'd been so young and scared and hurt. She convinced herself that his absence didn't matter, but hearing him now, she realized that the pregnancy and loss of their baby did matter to Reese as much as it did to her.

"Do you...do you think you lost our son because I caused you a lot of stress?"

"*No*." Nina twisted around to face him and cupped his right jaw. A frown lined his brow. "Losing him wasn't my fault, and it wasn't your fault."

"I know that stress can cause problems when a woman is pregnant."

"That's not what happened."

"Is that what the doctor said?" he asked, doubtful and carrying a burden that no one should bear.

"Women miscarry all the time, sometimes before they know they're pregnant. It happens. I miscarried a couple of months after we broke up, so it had nothing to do with you."

Her thumb rubbed his cheekbone, and she kissed the spot on the bridge of his nose where the freckles congregated.

"Don't carry that burden. It wasn't your fault. I promise."

Reese rolled onto his back and pulled her on top of him. He smoothed a hand up and down her spine.

"It'll be daybreak soon, and then we'll have to get up." She whispered the words against his collarbone.

"I'm going to call into work. Let's not do anything today."

"I'll call in, too, but what will we do all day?"

"Stay in bed, watch movies, order room service. What do you say?"

He kissed her temple, and she burrowed deeper into his embrace and shut her eyes. For today at least, she didn't want to think.

At some point, Nina knew she would have to face her actions. But not now.

She smiled. "I like that idea."

CHAPTER 22

*R*eese woke up on Tuesday morning with Nina rubbing her butt against him.

He sheathed his shaft and entered her from behind, and she let out a soft moan. Damn, the sound of her pleasure was its own aphrodisiac. He squeezed her breasts together, and she grew slicker, arching her back and sliding her ass back and forth against him.

His breathing became laborious as he pressed his face to the side of her neck and kept squeezing the fullness of her breasts, massaging and rubbing the hard nipples.

She reached back for a kiss, which he gave. Then she turned away, but he put a hand at the upper part of her throat and twisted her head back to him. Her eyes were closed, lashes on her cheeks, biting her lip. His hard thigh sliced between her softer ones, and he slowly moved his hips as she took her pleasure.

Then her orgasm hit, and her lips parted, and she gyrated faster against him, and he gritted his teeth, fighting back his release so he could watch her come undone. She gasped, followed by a soft wail. When she finished, he grabbed her hips and thrust faster until he climaxed with his head pressed to the back of her neck.

He wanted to wake up like this every morning. Nuzzling her neck, he kept them together with his thigh between her legs. "I'm stuck."

Nina giggled softly. "Behave."

He kissed her neck. "Okay." He sighed. "Guess I'll get up, but not because I want to."

He'd had a change of clothes delivered last night because he and Nina hadn't left her apartment one time yesterday. He couldn't skip another day of work, and Nina had to go to hotel headquarters to make the announcement that she was accepting the position as CEO and Chairman of the Board and taking her rightful place at the helm of the company.

Reese rolled across the bed and planted his feet on the floor.

"You go first. I'm staying in bed a little longer," Nina mumbled into the pillow.

"You better get up, or you'll be late." Reese walked around the bed toward the bathroom but hung back at the door to watch her.

Nina was buried under covers pulled up to her neck. Her eyes were closed, and she looked peaceful and content—and he felt the same. His mind was finally at ease. All this time, the regret of their broken relationship had never left him. He'd lived with that feeling so long that it had been a part of him, stitched into his DNA, until now. The past twenty-four hours cleared his mind, and he was finally at peace.

Nina was his everything. His life's blood. The beginning, the end, and all in-between.

And she was finally back where she belonged, with him, and he planned to keep it that way.

Reese went into the bathroom to take his shower.

* * *

NINA CHECKED her appearance one more time in the full-length mirror in the walk-in closet. She'd changed outfits three times and finally settled on a black pants suit with a black belt and three-quarter length sleeves. The light fabric was comfortable, and wearing black made her feel powerful.

She wore her hair pulled back and had removed the stud from her nose and inserted a nose retainer before applying her makeup. She only wore a few pieces of jewelry—earrings and a silver charm bracelet on her left wrist. Her good-luck charm because it was a gift from her father.

Patting her stomach, she hoped the single slice of toast stayed down. She was so wired about today. She'd called a meeting to announce her decision to take her rightful position in the company. If anyone had told her a year ago that she'd make such a significant step, she'd tell them they were crazy, but this was the right decision, the decision her father had wanted her to make, and the role in which she could have the greatest impact.

She teared up when she thought about how proud he would be that The Winthrop Helping Hands Program was successful and would be implemented company-wide. Overall, she had a lot to learn, and not everyone was happy she'd returned. But she had the support of most of the staff, and the consultants would help implement the changes she wanted to make. She had Reese's support, too.

While she was confident about the direction her professional life was going in, she wasn't so sure about the direction of her personal one. The past day with Reese had been heaven, where they spent the entire day and night in her apartment watching television, talking, and making love. An ideal twenty-four hours, but she had to face reality at some point.

If she thought too long about what was happening, she became emotional and scared about her predicament. What was she doing with Reese, and how would that affect her relationship with Andy, whom she'd barely thought about the entire time? When he agreed to a break, she hadn't expected to sleep with anyone else and was certain that had not been on Andy's mind, either.

"How are you holding up?" Reese asked from the doorway, looking handsome in a slimming navy Italian suit.

"I'm a little nervous," Nina admitted with a shaky laugh.

"You got this." He walked over and stood behind her. The scent of his aftershave filled the space between them and tickled her nose. Placing his hands on her shoulders, he said, "Repeat after me: This is my goddamn company."

"Reese, I don't want to do this," Nina whined.

"Repeat. After. Me. This is my goddamn company."

Nina sighed dramatically. "This is my goddamn company."

"Say it like you mean it."

"I feel silly."

"*Say it.*" He glared at her in the mirror.

Nina straightened her shoulders and stood straight. "This is *my* goddamn company."

"And I'm the CEO."

"And I'm the CEO," she said with a little more attitude and a neck roll.

"And I got this."

"And I got this."

"Perfect." Reese pulled her back by the waist and placed a loud smack on her cheek. "You're gonna knock 'em dead, baby."

Minutes later, they were both ensconced in the back seat of her Mercedes. Nina was going to drop Reese at work first since her meeting didn't start until ten o'clock.

"You're so late," she said.

He looked completely unconcerned. "I'll just tell my mother the woman she loves more than me made me late, and all should be fine."

"Don't say that!"

He chuckled and squeezed her hand.

They pulled up in front of the SJ Brands building, and Reese said, "You should come in and say hi. I'm sure everybody would love to see you."

"It's not a good idea." He was reaching for more than she could readily offer right now, trying to establish their relationship in a way that left her floundering because she wasn't sure what exactly they were doing.

"Why not?" He must have recognized her discomfort because he immediately followed up with, "Another time. Don't forget you got this. Call and let me know how everything went. If I need to come up to Winthrop headquarters and kick some ass, let me know." He leaned in and gave her a quick kiss goodbye.

Nina turned away from watching him walk into the building. She hunched down in the seat and fought back tears. She didn't know why she wanted to cry. She enjoyed sleeping with Reese, but everything could easily get out of control. He wanted more, and she wasn't sure she could give it to him. Could she take the leap?

"Philippe, could you drive around for a bit, please?" she asked hoarsely.

"Yes, ma'am."

What am I doing?

She and Andy were on a break, but *she* needed to face the truth—how quickly she'd jumped at his suggestion that they take a week or two off from their relationship. One week or two, he'd asked. She'd chosen two weeks—the longer period. Maybe Reese was what she'd wanted all along. She'd fought her attraction to him, but the break gave her the excuse she'd needed. She had to make a decision, but whatever the choice, someone would get hurt.

Nina let out a tremulous sigh, and tears tumbled onto her

cheeks. *I'm falling apart*, she thought, rubbing the tears from her eyes with the heels of her hands.

"Ma'am?"

Philippe extended a handkerchief over the back of the seat. Their eyes met in the rearview mirror, and she saw nothing but compassion there.

"Thank you." She took the handkerchief.

Without being asked, the driver rolled up the partition and allowed her to cry in private.

* * *

NINA SPENT thirty minutes in her father's old office—now her office—preparing for the meeting. During that period, she made up her mind that as far as she and Reese were concerned, she didn't have to make a decision yet. She had ten days left in her break from Andy.

She and the two consultants made their way to the conference room, where members of the board and executive-level staff had gathered. As soon as they entered, the hum of conversation silenced.

With more confidence than she felt, she walked to the head of the conference table and set down the folder tucked under her arm. She remained standing and let her gaze sweep the room. Some of the staff sat in chairs, and others stood at the back and off to the side. Some liked her, some didn't, others were politely distant, but they all wanted to hear what The Heir had to say.

She took a fortifying breath. She was twenty-nine years old and taking the helm of a multimillion-dollar company.

This is my goddamn company.

I'm the CEO.

I got this.

"Good morning." She broke into a smile.

"Good morning," the group echoed back.

Nina placed her hands on the leather chair in front of her. "I was very pleased with the results of the Helping Hands project. I want to publicly thank all of you for your assistance in the testing phase and for pulling together the data. A very special thank-you to Janice Livingston and Nathan Crenshaw, who crunched the numbers and made me very, very happy."

She clapped her hands, and the rest of them followed suit. Nathan was the vice-president of finance for the entire company, and Janice was the regional vice-president of finance for the east coast hotels. The pilot program had been rolled out in Janice's territory, overseen by Nathan. They both sat near the back, Janice in a pale-rose dress and matching glasses. She was an interesting character, and Nina looked forward to getting to know her. Anyone who managed to find frames to fit all their colorful outfits had to be fun.

The clapping died down, and Nina spoke again, keeping her voice steady. "We're going to implement the program company-wide, and the consultants and I have worked on ideas we'll be going over with the appropriate team members. However, the main reason I asked you all to be here this morning was because I have a very important announcement to make." Her voice became stronger the longer she spoke. "I have decided to accept the position of CEO and Chairman of the Board, effective immediately, so there are going to be a few changes around here."

CHAPTER 23

*G*roggily, Nina reached for the vibrating phone on the bedside table. Squinting, she peeked at the screen and saw Andy's name. The second time he'd called today. She had ignored the earlier call while she and Reese were out to dinner. He hadn't left a voice mail or sent a text, but since he was calling again, she wondered if something was wrong.

Casting a quick glance at Reese's sleeping form, Nina answered in a quiet voice. "Hello?"

"Hi, Nina. It's me, Andy."

She eased from under Reese's arm and tiptoed across the carpet to the bathroom.

"Hi." She kept her voice low.

"I called earlier." He didn't say anything else, clearly expecting her to explain herself.

"Did you? I had the ringer turned off," she said, though that didn't explain why she'd put off calling him back.

"Oh."

Andy didn't say anything more for several seconds, during which Nina eased the door almost closed behind her, leaving it slightly ajar.

"How have you been?" Andy asked.

"Good." Nina didn't know what else to say—and she didn't know the purpose of the call.

She sat down on the edge of the large tub. The city lights winked at her through the one-way window.

"It's been a week."

"Yeah."

"What have you been up to?"

"Um, busy at work. We started the rollout of the volunteer program and picked a candidate to oversee it. That person will report directly to me because I took over as CEO of the company."

"You did?" Utter shock filled his voice.

"I can head up The Winthrop Hotel Group and be a wife and mother. I can do all three."

"It's not easy to do, Nina."

"If I have support, it would be."

She waited for him to respond. When he finally did, there was no inflection in his voice. "You're right, women can have it all, just like men."

She wasn't sure if he was serious or merely stating what he thought she wanted to hear.

Andy let out a sigh. "Listen, I don't want us to argue. I called because I understand that you needed this break, but I miss you and hope you can forgive me."

"I have a lot to digest," Nina said, staring at her toes.

"I know, but I want you to remember all the good times we had. Remember the good times? Working on the farm was hard labor, but I enjoyed it. Working with the disabled women in India was also a highlight of the trip. Being able to give back to the world we live in is not only important, it's imperative. I believe in your vision. If we all do our share, we could make this world an even better place to live. I want to be part of that with you, Nina.

"I know I've been busy since our return to the States, but my schedule won't always be like that. Once work settles down in New York, I won't have to travel as much, and I'll have more time. Then I can help with your projects here, like feeding the hungry, building homes, or whatever you have going on. I want to do those things. I want us to raise our children with that type of awareness and desire to do good."

He pushed all the right buttons, said everything she wanted to hear.

"Keep that in mind?" Andy said.

"I will."

"And keep in mind how much I miss you, and how much I love you, and how much I need you. You're my rock. When my mother passed, you were there for me in a way no one else was, and I still need you, Nina."

Her face crumbled as she fought back tears.

"Don't give up on us yet, okay?"

Nina held the phone to her chest and took a breath that shook with emotion, and then she placed it back to her ear. "Okay," she said softly.

Andy sighed with relief. "I'm gonna let you go. Have a good night. I miss you."

"Good night." Nina hung up but kept her gaze lowered, eyes resting unseeingly at the floor.

Reese or Andy? Should she throw away her steady, safe relationship with Andy for the emotional highs she experienced with Reese right now? Should she forego the possibility of marriage and children with a man who wanted to give her both, for a man she was too afraid to broach the subject with, for fear his answer would be the same as before and crush her spirits?

She still had seven days to go before she had to make a decision. She stood and let out a cry of surprise at the sight of Reese filling the open door, bare-chested and in boxers. Shadow covered his face, which made it impossible to read his expression.

"Who was that?" he asked.

Nina clutched the phone to her chest. "Andy."

"What did he want?" The lack of emotion in his voice chilled her.

"He wanted to check on me and see how I was doing."

"In the middle of the fucking night?" No mistaking his anger.

Reese walked closer, and she saw his face better. He shot a furious glance at the phone in her hand. "How about this? The next time he calls, give *me* the phone. I'll tell him how you're doing."

He pulled her closer and kissed her hard. She tasted fury and jealousy in the kiss, and although she knew it was his way of placing a stamp on her, she enjoyed it. He grabbed her ass with both hands and lifted her from the floor.

His hard length nudged her core, and as the kiss deepened, she let out a soft sigh.

In the bedroom, he took her hard. The curly hairs on his thighs rubbed against the sensitive insides of her legs, creating the most delicious friction as the full weight of him pressed her into the mattress with each deep stroke. He kissed and sucked on her neck with ruthless vigor and would surely leave hickeys on her skin, but she didn't care. She wanted to be marked by him.

Their frantic pace harkened her orgasm that much sooner. Her loins erupted with pleasure, and her fingers sank into his tight ass. Shuddering through the climax, she sank her heels into the bed and launched her hips faster and upward to grasp every ounce of pleasure he offered.

Reese trembled above her, his head dropping to her shoulder as his own orgasm claimed him. He drove deeper, breath coming in short, desperate pants that beat against the tops of her breasts.

After a long exhale, he lay still and spent on top of her. Nina closed her eyes, thoroughly satisfied after one of the most intense orgasms she'd had in recent memory.

* * *

NINA ROLLED over in the empty bed. "Reese?" she called.

No response and no light under the bathroom door. The apartment was completely quiet.

"Reese?"

Still no response.

She slipped from the bed and found her discarded clothes from earlier. She put on the cami top and her boy shorts and went in search of Reese.

She found him in what he called the workroom, and she watched him work, mumbling to himself as he tapped the keyboard in front of him at a long table littered with computer parts and laptops in various stages of disassembly.

Standing in the doorway, she had the answer to the question that had tortured her the past few days. She wanted Reese, even if she couldn't have every item on her wish list.

No matter how hard she tried, she couldn't sever the rope that tied them together. She broke off contact with him for over a year, but he roped her back in. She ran from him for three years, terrified by the power of a single kiss, yet here she was—in his apartment, sharing his bed, loving him in a way she loved no one else.

She loved Andy, but what she felt for him didn't compare to what she felt for Reese. She fell for Andy slowly, without drama and fireworks. But Reese was a pyrotechnic display on the Fourth of July, a raging river with twists and turns that kept her guessing and excited.

She couldn't call that love. Love was insufficient a term to sum up the extent of the marrow-deep emotion that consumed her. It was deeper than love.

And as much as she hated to hurt Andy, she couldn't go through life without Reese. Because for so long, there had been a hole in her heart that never healed, and opening herself to the possibility of a future together had finally fixed it.

Nina walked on quiet feet across the carpet and placed her hands on Reese's shoulders.

He glanced back at her. "Hey," he said.

She pressed two soft kisses to his freckled shoulder and flung her arms around his neck so they were cheek to cheek. "I don't want to bother you," she said, though that was exactly what she was doing.

His fingers encircled one of her wrists. "You're not. I need a break anyway. Come here."

He pulled her around in front of him and across his lap. Nina wrapped her arms around his neck. "I'm sorry about earlier. It won't happen again," she said.

She dreaded the talk she needed to have with Andy, but she would set one up between them as soon as his schedule allowed. She didn't want to hurt him. She knew what it was like to bear the brunt of someone else's rejection and didn't want to be that person, but it was time for her to move on.

Reese's jaw clenched. "Talk to him. Or I will."

"I'll talk to him," she said. His shoulders relaxed, and she moved on to a topic he'd enjoy much more. "What are you working on?"

A smile broke out on his face. "Honestly, it's top-secret, but I'll share it with you."

"Oh, my, I feel special."

He laughed. Rubbing a hand up and down her bare thigh, he launched into a detailed explanation of the proprietary software he was working on for SJ Brands. "Right now, it's in the beginning stages, and I'm only able to work on it in my spare time, but the idea is to have one piece of software that seamlessly incorporates inventory management, channel management, and forecasting."

"Doesn't software like that already exist?"

His smile broadened. "Yes, but mine will be better."

He explained the technicalities, the drawbacks of using other software, and the benefits he anticipated coming from his own. He tried to simplify the jargon, but much of the explanation went over her head.

When he finished, all she said was, "Oh, okay."

"I lost you, didn't I?" he asked.

"Kinda," Nina admitted.

Reese laughed. "I still have a lot of work to do. Might take another year or so, but it's definitely coming."

"I don't want to keep you from your work. I know how much you enjoy your problem-solving, so I'll leave you alone now. I just wanted a quick snuggle." Nina pulled in close to him again, inhaled his skin, and then kissed him briefly on the lips.

"Good night," she said.

"Good night."

She stood and went to the door but paused before walking out. Reese was already engrossed in his work, and knowing him, he would be there for a few more hours, probably not coming to bed until he saw the light of dawn outside.

This was their future. This type of normalcy—the warm, fuzzy feeling that broke through the hard shell of her heart.

No doubt about it. Her future was with Reese.

* * *

NINA LOOKED across the breakfast table at Reese, who frowned at his phone.

"What's wrong?" she asked.

"I received a message from the IT team that the system is down. I need to go in there early. Crap."

"Duty calls."

He smiled wryly at her across the table. "Unfortunately, that means I need to leave now. I hoped for a leisurely breakfast with you."

She reached across the table and interlocked their fingers together. "It's fine. I'll see you later tonight."

"I have to stop by Ella's tonight after work, so I'll be a little late."

"No problem. I'll see you at my place later when you get through." In a short period, she'd gotten used to them bouncing from one apartment to the next.

Reese stood and gave her a lingering kiss. He cupped her jaw gently, like holding fragile glass. "I could get used to this," he whispered against her lips.

Then he was gone, and Nina sat there reminiscing on his words.

She could get used to this, too.

CHAPTER 24

*H*e couldn't lose her again. This time, their relationship had to work.

Reese rocked back and forth in his leather chair, staring with unseeing eyes at the buildings laid out before him. Andy's call angered him. He represented a problem that Reese hadn't resolved.

Reese hadn't asked Nina about her relationship status with Andy, and she hadn't offered an explanation. All he knew was that she no longer wore her ring, and she and Reese spent all their spare time together and regularly made love.

He had assumed she and Andy were finished, but he wasn't so sure. She had history with him, recent history that could prove problematic. Reese needed to strengthen his position by taking a step he'd considered for some time, but it was now imperative to do. He couldn't let that snake shimmy his way back between them, so he'd do what he should have done years ago.

Reese took the hall to Ella's office. Being Friday, half the employees had already left, and he was on his way out, too.

He knocked on the doorframe, and she looked up. "I'm

leaving a little early," he informed her. "I'm going to stop by and say good night to Mother before I go."

"She already left." Ella set down her pen. "Where are you headed?"

"I have an errand to run."

"Errand? You're being very evasive." Her eyes came alive with curiosity.

"Don't worry, you'll find out the details soon enough." His family would be ecstatic when he and Nina became engaged.

"Now you've really piqued my interest, but I'll be patient."

He laughed, in the best mood he'd been in since...since he couldn't remember when. That's how he knew this decision was the right one. "See you later."

He took the elevator to the first floor where a private car sent by Klopard Jewelers waited for him. The unmarked vehicle took him through the streets of Atlanta and dropped him in front of the high-end jewelers' main retail store.

When Reese stepped inside, the host greeted him, chief gemologist Casper Jones, a slight man with a wiry build and an almost meek posture.

He extended a pale, thin hand and shook Reese's hand firmly. "Mr. Brooks, nice to meet you in person."

"I'm excited to see what you have to show me," he said to Casper.

"I think you'll be pleased. Follow me."

This was not the first time Casper had worked with the family, but it was the first time he'd worked with Reese.

After Andy called last night, Reese knew he had to move quickly to show Nina he was serious about their relationship and eliminate Andy from her life for good.

He was going to ask her to marry him, a man who at one time doubted he'd ever get married. He wanted to wake up next to her every morning, just like he had every morning since they first made love. All he could think about was the two of them raising a family together, and it didn't terrify him.

They took the elevator to the top of the building and stepped out onto a floor made of Belgian marble. The private salon was located behind two large doors covered in fake gemstones, which Casper pulled open. Reese followed him into the quiet residential-looking interior decorated in a white-and-cream-color palette. A few signature pieces of jewelry were on display beneath glass, but for the most part, the choices were locked away.

"Can I get you something to drink?" Casper asked.

Reese shook his head. "I'm good."

The jeweler took a seat behind a white desk, and Reese sat down in the armchair opposite him. Casper flicked on a lamp and then removed a tray from the desk. Three diamond rings rested on the black fabric.

Casper went through a brief explanation about each and then asked, "What do you think?"

They were huge, as Reese had requested, because he wanted a gemstone larger than the one Andy had given Nina.

"This is the biggest one you have?" he asked, pointing at the one in the middle.

"We can go bigger, but based on your description of your future fiancée, this might be the better piece for you." Casper held up the first one.

Reese took the ring and studied it under the light. It was a beautiful ring, exactly the type of jewelry Nina deserved, but the diamond wasn't big enough. None of them were.

"I want you to go bigger," he said, setting it down.

"Bigger?"

He looked steadily at Casper. "Bigger. Of course, I can go elsewhere if you can't accommodate me."

Casper laughed softly. "I assure you, Mr. Brooks, we can accommodate you. If we don't have what you're looking for here, we can certainly acquire it for you. But please, give me a moment. I believe I have something that you'll like."

Casper disappeared and left Reese alone. He returned with a satisfied smile on his face. Inside a glass box, nestled in white silk, was the largest diamond Reese had ever laid his eyes on.

"What do you think about this?" Casper opened the box and set it in front of Reese before taking a seat. He went into the specifics, detailing the origin of the stone, the cut, and the number of carats.

Turning it over in his hand, Reese admired its radiance and clarity. "Perfect. How much?"

"Three and a half million."

"I'll take it. This stone, with that setting, with one change." They went over the details for Nina's ring and the wedding bands, and Casper promised they'd start on the designs right away.

At the end of the meeting, both men shook hands, and Reese exited the building, knowing he'd made the right decision.

He declined Klopard's offer of a ride back, opting to go nearby and pick up dinner to go. Then he'd order a car to take him back to Nina's tonight.

He pulled out his phone to call her and see if she wanted him to bring her something to eat.

"Hi, Reese."

He turned in the direction of a woman's voice.

Chelsea was standing on the sidewalk. He hadn't seen her since he left her in the suite at the Ritz Carlton, but she had called once and informed him that she and her boyfriend had reconciled.

"Hey, you." He gave her a hug. "What are you doing in Atlanta?"

"Apartment hunting."

"Are you leaving New York?" he asked, surprised.

Chelsea sighed heavily. "I need a change of pace. Things didn't quite work out with me and my boyfriend."

"Damn. I'm sorry to hear that."

She shrugged, though he saw pain flicker in her eyes. "My biological clock is ticking, and I don't have time to waste on him anymore. What are you getting into?"

"Headed home," Reese replied.

"Can you spare a few minutes to have a drink with a friend?"

"I, uh..." Reese glanced at his watch. Nina expected him to be late, so he could afford to kill thirty minutes or so by having a drink with Chelsea. "Yeah, I could do that."

"Good. You're buying, and I'm whining," she said, slipping an arm through his.

"I feel like I'm getting the raw end of this deal."

Laughing, they walked off in the direction of a lounge nearby where they could grab a drink.

* * *

THE DOOR CREAKED, and Nina's eyes popped open. She had dozed off with a management book on her chest.

"Hey," she greeted Reese, stretching her hands above her head.

"Hi," he said.

She glanced at the bedside clock. "I didn't know when you said you were going to be late, you meant this late. It's after nine o'clock."

"Sorry about that. Had a million things to do."

"Everything okay with Ella and Tyrone and the girls?"

"What?" Reese looked confused.

"You said you were going over to Ella's after work, right?"

"Oh, yeah. Everything is fine with them," he said dismissively.

He walked toward the bathroom.

"Hey, don't I get a kiss?"

He paused. "I would, but I smell bad from running around with the kids, getting sweaty with the dog and all that. Let me take a quick shower, and I'll greet you properly." He flashed a grin and winked, but the whole exchange seemed forced.

Sensing something amiss, Nina watched him go into the bathroom.

A few minutes later, she swung her legs off the bed and walked to the door. She eased it open and listened to the sound of the shower running, and saw Reese behind the beveled glass of the stall.

She entered, casting a cursory glance at the clothes piled on the floor—jacket, shirt, slacks, and undershirt. A small wet spot near the left pocket of his pants, which had been hidden by his jacket when he came into the bedroom, caught her eye. She nudged the pants with her toe, revealing a larger spot than she originally thought.

She walked over and opened the stall door. Reese had his face upturned into the spray of the shower, water running down his muscular body—biceps, tight thighs, and his firm ass.

He started when he saw her. "Hey."

"Did you spill something on your clothes?" Nina asked.

He frowned, as if the question confused him. "Er..."

"Your pants are wet."

"Oh, yeah, one of the kids spilled something on me," Reese replied.

"Is everything okay?" Nina asked.

"Yeah. Everything is fine."

He didn't seem to be lying, but he seemed off. She couldn't put her finger on exactly why.

"Okay."

Reese extended his hand, and she took it, stepping into the shower with him.

"You know I love you, right?"

That was unexpected. She swallowed hard. Water pummeled her hair and soaked her camisole and underwear.

"Yes." He didn't ask for reciprocation, and she was afraid to say the words.

"You don't have to say it. I already know." His face broke into a wide grin before he kissed her hard with such passion, he left her breathless. "I want to give you the world, Nina," he whispered huskily against her lips.

Maybe she couldn't say the words yet, but she could show him how much he meant to her. Greedily, Nina tasted his mouth and licked his neck while Reese deftly peeled the wet clothes from her body. They lathered each other's skin with soap, moving their hands in sensual, circular motions that aroused as much as they cleaned.

After they dried off from the shower, Reese backed her into the bedroom, and they made love. He lifted her legs onto his shoulders and lapped at the moisture between her legs until she came all over his mouth. Then his hard body pinned her to the mattress from behind, driving steadily into her as her whimpering cries bounced off the walls.

CHAPTER 25

*N*ina stood in the bathroom mirror, fluffing her hair with her fingers. For this evening's outing, she wore a black floral-print dress with a hemline landing above her knees. One of her favorite dresses because of the comfy elastic waist and full, long sleeves. Vintage chandelier earrings hung from her earlobes, and she tilted her head to the right, giving her reflection a critical assessment.

Beside her, Reese leaned back against the counter, looking casually stylish in a form-fitting white shirt, tan vest that hugged his chest, and dark slacks. He looked good, and he smelled good, too—the woodsy scent of his cologne lending its subtle aroma to the air.

"Does my hair look okay?" she asked.

Reese glanced up from his phone. "Better than okay. Your hair looks great and you look beautiful."

"You're so full of it. You're just ready to go." She pursed her lips.

"I'm serious. You know you're beautiful," he said with a soft smile.

"You get a kiss for that." She stood on tiptoe, pressed her lips against his, and slipped in a little tongue.

Reese's arm immediately snaked around her waist and he deepened the kiss, pressing his mouth harder against hers and using firm strokes of his tongue.

Nina pressed a hand to his chest. "We don't have time for this," she whispered against the corner of his mouth.

Reese bit his lip and looked down at her with half-closed eyes. "You sure? I'll be in and out before you know it."

She giggled. "If that's the case, I'll be mad, so the answer is definitely no." He groaned and she pulled away. "We have to go or we'll be late."

"Fine."

As she did one final check of her appearance, Reese pinched her butt.

Nina hopped away and fake glared. "Quit," she said.

"Don't throw it in my face then." He braced his sturdy arms on either side of her on the counter.

"I didn't." She laughed and threw her arms around his waist. She gazed at his handsome face, eyes traveling over his freckled nose, hard jaw, and his tempting lips before lifting to his eyes. The smile slowly died on her face.

"Sometimes I can't believe you're here. Feel like I'm dreaming," he whispered.

She did too, and was afraid to wake up and have to face reality without him. What she felt for him was so new after hiding behind her fears for so long. Their relationship had to last this time. She'd break apart if she lost him again.

"You're not. We're not," she said quietly.

Their lips met in a tender, affectionate kiss that shuttled away the fear in her heart and replaced it with possibilities for a bright future. When they broke apart, Reese held her chin between his thumb and forefinger.

"You don't get to leave again."

"I'm never going anywhere else without you," Nina promised softly.

"Good." He sighed. "Let's go before I change my mind about going out."

Reese had surprised her with tickets to the Alvin Ailey performance at the Fox Theatre downtown. She hadn't been to a show in years and greatly anticipated seeing their graceful moves on stage.

When they arrived at his Mercedes in the underground parking lot, Nina expected Reese to open the passenger door and let her in, but instead, he dangled the keys in front of her.

"You get to drive today," he said.

She gasped. "I do?" She reached for the keys, but he snatched them back and closed his fingers around them like a Venus flytrap.

"There are conditions," Reese said ominously.

"Okay," Nina said slowly.

"First, you drive the speed limit."

She could do that. "No problem." She anxiously bounced on her toes.

"Second, no huffing and puffing and no honking the horn because other drivers, in your words, 'don't know what they're doing.'"

"You're stifling my ability to express myself!" she exclaimed.

"And no cursing."

"What? Come on, you're being ridiculous."

"Do you want to drive the Mercedes or not?"

She seriously reconsidered, but then glanced at its shiny golden exterior and remembered the leather seats and wood grain interior, and her obstinance disintegrated.

"I do," she muttered.

"So we have a deal? None of the above?"

"None of the above," she grumbled.

Reese extended the keys and she snatched them away. "You're a jerk," she said.

"Hey, I can still take those back."

He took a step toward her and Nina ran around the car. With much laughter, she hopped in the driver's seat. Reese sent another warning look as he climbed in the passenger side.

Nina ignored him and adjusted the seat and steering wheel and started the engine. The vehicle purred to life, and she caressed the circumference of the wheel. "She sounds so good," she moaned.

Reese bit his lip as he watched her. "Keep doing that and you'll make me fuck you in this car again."

Nina batted her eyelashes at him. "Promises, promises." She pulled out of the parking space, and he laughed softly.

She did well most of the way, adhering to the rules under his watchful eye, but as they neared the Fox Theatre and the bottle-neck of cars caused by the show, someone abruptly swung into her lane, and Nina slammed on the brakes.

She hit the steering wheel. "Look at this assho—" She broke off and glanced guiltily at Reese and finished more quietly. "I mean, look at this gentleman who clearly doesn't know how to drive."

Reese burst out laughing. "You were so close to getting through the trip without cursing."

"Ugh. It's so hard."

"You get one," he said, lifting a single finger and showing her mercy.

"Thank you," Nina said gratefully. Then she glared at the offending car. "Asshole!"

Reese cracked up some more.

Not long after, they took their seats in the crowded theater and settled in for the show. At least five years had passed since Nina had seen an Alvin Ailey production, and the performance surpassed her memories and made her feel as if she were a first-time attendee.

Enthralled, she couldn't take her eyes from the stage. The mostly Black dancers had such grace and style, their muscles rippling as they contorted their backs into tight bows, their hands into twisting arcs, and their bodies into flying vessels as they moved through the air in eye-catching costumes. Decades after Ailey's death, they continued to express the stories he wanted told about Black pain but also Black celebration, emotional but uplifting tales portrayed through the vehicle of modern dance.

Reese arranged for her to meet the dancers after the show, and Nina got to chat with them and take pictures. She was still in a sense of euphoria as they strolled out of the venue. Reese took her hand in his and shifted their positions so she was on the inside of the sidewalk, and he walked on the street side.

"That was wonderful," she sighed. "I wish I'd taken dance classes so I could understand a little bit of what it means to move like that and tell stories with my body." She took several steps on her toes.

"It's not too late," Reese said, smiling and twirling her in a circle.

Nina squeezed his arm and rested her temple against his left arm. "Nah, it's too late, but I can dream."

"You had a different calling, babe. You're going to help so many people with the work you and your staff do."

"Yeah."

People who'd left the show crowded the sidewalk. Walking slowly, Reese and Nina went along with the flow of pedestrian foot traffic. There was no rush because there would be a horrendous gridlock on Peachtree Street for a while. Cars crept by with the occasional one blowing its horn, barely moving, a typical Saturday night in downtown Atlanta with people attending different functions, going to, and leaving from, dinners and shows and whatever else was taking place in the city.

Nina looked up at Reese and threaded her fingers through his. "I had a great time."

His gaze was filled with love. That was the only way to describe his expression and the way his eyes held hers. "Good," was all he said as they made their way to the car.

* * *

REESE SWALLOWED his vitamins with a mouthful of water and then turned out the light in the kitchen. He entered the bedroom in time to see Nina exiting the bathroom where she'd been twisting her hair. She had secured the plaits with a silk scarf and glanced at him as he came in. While he wore the pajama bottoms, she wore the shirt of the set, which looked much better on her than it had ever looked on him.

"Did you take your vitamins?" he asked.

"Oh, shoot. I forgot."

He handed her the half full glass of water, and she removed the pills from her purse and swallowed them down. Reese climbed into bed as she placed the empty glass on the nightstand.

"I've gotta do better about remembering to take those things," Nina said.

"Set a reminder, like I do," Reese said.

Nina turned off the light and climbed into bed, too. She scooted toward him in the middle. "You set a reminder for your vitamins but not your mother's birthday?"

"Don't judge me."

"I'm just saying..." She gave him a quick kiss and then turned onto her side. He pulled her closer so they could spoon.

"You still meeting your mother for brunch tomorrow?"

Nina groaned. "Yes, unfortunately. I thought about canceling to come see you play, but I promised I'd meet her, so..." She shrugged.

"You can see me whoop some ass another time." Reese and some friends were playing football in the park.

Nina shifted and her soft bottom pushed up against him. He groaned, slipping a knee between her thighs. "Stop trying to seduce me. I gave you some dick before we went to the show. That's it for the night. I'm cutting you off."

She giggled. He loved to make her laugh.

"I'm not trying to get any more dick, thank you very much."

They were quiet for a few minutes, and he thought she might have fallen asleep.

"I wonder what she wants," Nina said.

"Who?"

"My mother."

"What makes you think she wants something?"

She didn't answer for a while, and then she said, "She always wants something."

He hated to hear the sound of hurt in her voice and squeezed her a little tighter. "I'm sorry, babe."

"She's not all bad, and I know she loves me, it's just...I don't know. She's never satisfied. Did I ever tell you that my dad provided for her in his will?"

"No, you never mentioned it." That surprised him since her parents had divorced long before her father died.

"He did."

"And she still asks you for money?"

"Yeah. Never satisfied," Nina said with an air of defeat.

"You need to be strong when you're dealing with her."

"I know." She played with one of his fingers. "But she's my mom, and it's hard, you know?"

"I know."

"And it's not like I can't afford her requests, so...you know what, I'm not going to worry about it. Maybe she wants to get together for mother-daughter time, that's all," Nina said.

That sounded like wishful thinking, but Reese didn't want to say too much because as Nina pointed out, Gloria was her mother, and he was fiercely loyal to his own family. He just didn't like to see Nina upset, and since Gloria had never liked him, there was no love lost between him and her. As far as he was concerned, he could live his life quite happily without ever seeing Nina's mother again, but she was Nina's only living parent, and Nina held on to that relationship tightly and with both hands.

"I'm sure you'll have a great brunch. If you don't, when you come back I'll give you one of my relaxing massages," Reese said.

"Mmm, that sounds good. Promise?"

"Promise. Go to sleep, babe." He kissed the back of her neck.

"Good night."

CHAPTER 26

"Hi, honey." Gloria gave Nina a hug and then stepped back to examine her appearance. "You look nice. I like your hair."

She'd done another twist-out. "Thanks. You look great, too. Those colors look good on you," Nina said, referring to the floral print dress her mother wore.

"Thank you. My face is so dry, though. Summer, fall, and winter are my enemies." Gloria sat down.

Nina sat opposite her at the round table. "So spring is the only season that you like?"

"The only one," Gloria confirmed with a laugh.

The waiter came over. "What can I get for you lovely ladies?" he asked.

"Water and lemon for me, and I'll take the club sandwich," Nina said, closing the menu and handing it over.

"Water and lemon for me, as well, and I'll have the water-cress salad with chicken and the mustard vinaigrette." Gloria folded her menu and handed it to the waiter.

He disappeared, and Gloria smiled across the table at her. "How is work? Tell me everything."

Nina told her mother all about the Helping Hands Program and that she had taken over as CEO and Chairman of the Board.

Gloria's eyebrows pushed higher. "That's quite a switch from how you felt before when you didn't think that you could handle the responsibility."

"I've since decided that I can handle the responsibility," Nina said.

"Good for you. I'm very proud of you, and I'm sure your father would be, too, if he were here."

The waiter arrived with their waters, and after a brief question to ensure they didn't need anything, he disappeared again.

"I see you're not wearing your engagement ring. Anything you want to tell me?" Gloria folded her hands on the table.

That question must represent the real reason her mother had asked her to brunch. "I have a feeling you already know why I'm not wearing my ring. I'm sure Andy told you that he and I are on a break." Which would become permanent as soon as he returned from New York in a couple of days, and she could tell him face-to-face.

"You're right, I do know, but he didn't tell me. His father did."

"I didn't know you and Corbin were so close."

"We talk on occasion. After all, our children are getting married. Don't give me that look. I'm not in the market for a new husband. Those days are far behind me, and I've come to accept that marriage is not for me, and I'm perfectly fine living alone. Corbin called because he was concerned about Andy, who had been acting strangely, and he was finally able to get the truth out of him about your relationship. I don't pretend to understand the things that you young people do nowadays—breaks and all that. But Corbin did tell me that the break was your idea."

"I was upset because Andy lied to me."

"He's a man who was willing to do anything for you. Isn't

that what you want?"

Nina couldn't believe her mother was singing the same tired tune. "No, it's not, but that doesn't matter. The time apart has been good, and to be honest, has put things into perspective for me."

"What things?" Gloria asked.

Nina squeezed the lemon into her glass of water to buy time. "My relationship with Andy. I've been rethinking my expectations about the future."

"I see." Gloria folded her white napkin on the table and pressed down the edges with her hand. "Would your decision have anything to do with Reese Brooks and that hickey?"

Heat flamed Nina's cheeks, and she raised a hand to her neck. She'd worn her hair down to cover the bruise, but her mother still saw. At least she couldn't see the one on the swell of her right breast. "Yes, he and I are seeing each other again—as more than friends." She leaned forward in earnest. "Mom, I know you don't like him, but he's not a bad person. He has a lot of positive qualities, and he's changed since we were teenagers. I've changed, too."

Gloria smiled tightly. "That's quite a ringing endorsement."

"He's not the same selfish, untrustworthy person he was before." Convincing Gloria of his finer qualities would be a difficult task. Still, Nina wanted her mother to accept him and welcome him into the family the same way the Brooks family had always welcomed her.

"So he wants the same future that you do? Marriage, children?" The questions were spoken in a mocking tone.

Nina shifted. "I…"

"You haven't discussed the future with him, have you? Yet you're willing to throw away your future with Andy. And if Reese doesn't want what you want, are you willing to settle?" Gloria placed her hand over Nina's. "What do you think your father would say?"

Nina pulled her hand away. "Don't bring up my father."

"I only did because I know how much you valued his guidance and opinion, and he didn't approve of Reese. Andy is the kind of man your father would approve of."

"I'm not so sure about that. Andy wasn't completely honest with me, and I'm sure my father would not be pleased with his deception."

"Reese is much worse," Gloria said with much gravity in her voice. "You and Andy can build something together—a business, a family, a legacy. Reese is no good for you."

"He loves me."

"Love is a fallacy. Passion is fleeting."

"Lindsay found love and passion with Malik."

"We'll see how long that relationship lasts," Gloria said sarcastically. "How do you know he loves you?"

"He shows me. He told me."

"Again? The same way he loved you when he slept with a girl who hates you?"

"He said he didn't know."

"And you *believe* him?" Gloria looked and sounded appalled.

Nina squeezed her hands together in her lap in an effort to maintain control. She would not let her mother's bitterness stifle her happiness. "Is this why you invited me to brunch? Did Corbin send you here to convince me to ditch Reese and get back together with Andy?" Their meal would be cut short if that was the case.

"No one sends me to do anything. I'm here because you're my daughter, and I have very important information for you."

"And what information is that?"

Gloria grimaced. "I hate doing this, but I don't want you to make a mistake. Take a look at these pictures." She removed an envelope from her purse and shoved it across the table to Nina.

Nina stared at it, her body suddenly consumed with fear.

"Go ahead," Gloria nudged quietly.

"What is this?" Her voice shook.

"Look at them, Nina. Look at the man who you say loves you."

Slowly, she lifted her gaze to where her mother sat across the table. "I don't want to."

"You have to. You need to."

Gloria waited, and Nina listened to the other diners around her whisper-talking, the clatter of silverware on plates, and the burst of laughter from a group of friends seated near a window. They were happily living their lives, and she wanted to happily live hers, too. But when she opened the envelope, she knew that would change.

With trembling fingers, she pulled up the tab and slid out the photos. Four total, blown up to eight-by-ten images. One with Reese and a tall Black woman with long, straight hair walking down the street together arm in arm. One with them having drinks at a bar. He was laughing, and the woman had placed her hand on his arm and leaned closer.

In the third, Reese sat in the back of a car with the same woman straddling him. The last image showed them walking into a hotel, the woman leaning heavily on his arm.

"There were more, but I think you get the gist from these four. There's no need for overkill." Gloria spoke in a quiet voice.

Disbelief pounded into Nina like an avalanche of rocks, burying her under their weight.

"Where did you get these? Maybe it's not him." Her voice shook with the need for her statement to be true, no matter how ridiculous she sounded.

"You know that's him," her mother said gently.

Nina shook her head in denial. "It can't be. When were these taken? Maybe they're old," she said, grasping for any possibility that the photos were fake or a misunderstanding. Not Reese. Not after everything they'd shared the past week and a half.

"They were taken two nights ago and forwarded to me today."

Friday night, when he came in late and acted strange.

Nina looked at her mother, who was a blurry image behind the film of tears that covered her pupils. "This can't be right." Her breath hitched, and a tear fell from her eyes. She swiped it away quickly because once they started, she wouldn't be able to stop.

"It is right," Gloria said in the same gentle voice. Her face and body suggested concern, but she'd unleashed such devastating ugliness in the middle of a bright, beautiful day.

"He wouldn't," Nina said brokenly. Her lower lip trembled as tears flooded her cheeks. She didn't have the energy to wipe them away. "Why did you do this to me?"

Her mother's face softened with sympathy. "Because I don't want to see you get hurt. Because I don't want you to make a terrible mistake and choose the wrong man. Once I learned you and Andy were taking time away from your relationship, I knew you wouldn't stay away from Reese for long. I had him followed because I knew eventually he would slip up, and I was right. I'm sorry, honey. I know this isn't what you wanted to see, but sometimes the truth hurts. Is this the future that you want? Unmarried, no kids, and with your permanent boyfriend sleeping with any woman he wants to behind your back?

"Remember who he is. This is the man who slept with Kelly one week after he broke up with you and lied about it. And you were pregnant. He wasn't there to hold your hand. He wasn't there when my baby girl lay in a hospital bed suffering. Now this. He's not the man you want him to be."

Had he really deceived her? Was everything a lie? Nina couldn't feel anything. Pain had stripped away all sensation.

Gloria reached over and squeezed her trembling hand. "He is the same as he's always been. Honey, I love you, and you deserve so much better than Reese Brooks."

CHAPTER 27

*W*ith the phone against his ear, Reese hopped out of his Mercedes and rounded the front.

"Reese, I can't tell you enough how truly sorry I am. I'm so embarrassed," Chelsea said.

Reese took the ticket from the valet and entered The Winthrop Hotel. "Chelsea, I already told you it's fine. Quit apologizing. You'd been drinking, and in a bad place because of your breakup, so I'm not holding what happened Friday night against you."

"You should."

"I know you didn't mean any harm."

Misery leaked through the phone line with an exaggerated sigh from Chelsea. "You're too kind. The next time we get together, drinks are on me."

"Only if you behave."

She laughed. "Yes, and you can bring your girlfriend, that lucky bitch, to make sure I'm on my best behavior."

Reese nodded to several people in the elevator as he stepped on. "Her name is Nina, and if you're good, one day I'll let you meet her."

"Deal. Thank you for being such a sweetheart and not hating me for throwing myself, and the contents of my stomach, at you."

"Stop beating yourself up. We'll talk again soon."

They said goodbye to each other and hung up.

When the elevator doors opened, Reese stepped aside, and several people left. He migrated to the back and rested his head against the wall. After playing football in the park, he and his friends went out for drinks and talked trash to each other over appetizers.

On the way back from the pub, Chelsea called to apologize for throwing herself at him when they went to get drinks last Friday night. Despite their history, she had taken him by surprise with her aggressive behavior, but he recognized her actions were a cry for help because of the breakup. Their conversation had lasted longer than anticipated at the bar, but he could tell she had needed an ear.

Reese checked his phone as he stepped off the elevator on Nina's floor. He called earlier, but she never answered, and she hadn't responded to his text. He wondered if she was still with her mother.

He removed the key card from his wallet and stuck it in the door, turned the handle, and pushed. The door remained closed. Frowning, he examined the card to make sure he had pulled out the correct one. He re-inserted it into the slot and held it there a little longer. The lock whirred and clicked, but the light never changed from red to green.

"What the heck?" he muttered.

He wiped the magnetic strip in his T-shirt, probably not a good idea because the shirt was dirty and sweaty from playing football. He tried the door again. This time when it didn't open, he swore softly and headed back down the hallway toward the elevator. He rode to the first floor and went to the front desk, where he explained the situation and showed the clerk the card and his identification.

"I'm sorry, Mr. Brooks. One moment, please," she said with an apologetic smile. She punched a few keys, and then her forehead creased into a frown.

"What's the matter?" Reese started getting irritated. Whatever the malfunction with their system, he wanted it corrected right away so he could get upstairs and take a shower and change out of these clothes.

"I'm sorry, Mr. Brooks, but your key hasn't malfunctioned. It was deactivated, and we have a note here from Ms. Winthrop asking for a call should you come to the front desk." With an embarrassed smile, she picked up the phone and dialed.

What the heck is going on? Why would Nina authorize deactivating his key card?

The woman behind the counter extended the phone. "She wants to talk to you."

Reese accepted the receiver and turned his back to the Winthrop employee. He lowered his voice. "Babe, what's going on? You deactivated my card?"

"We need to talk." Her voice didn't contain any emotion, and alarm bells went off in his head.

"Where are you?" Reese asked.

"I'm upstairs."

"I was just up there trying to get in."

"I didn't hear you. You can come back up, and I'll let you in."

"Nina, what's going on?"

"I'll tell you when you get here." She hung up, and Reese stared at the receiver. Shaking out of his daze, he said, "Thank you," and handed back the phone to the woman behind the counter.

He made the return trip to Nina's apartment, and this time when he arrived, he knocked on the door.

Several seconds later, it opened, and Nina stood before him

with her hair in another cute twist out, a black shirt, and dark denim trousers. Reese entered cautiously, suspecting an ambush and completely in the dark about the reason.

They stood in the small space in front of the stairs. "What's wrong, Nina?"

"Let's talk in the living room."

He followed her up the stairs. He had anticipated the evening going a lot differently, figuring after a shower and a change of clothes, they would chill on the sofa and watch a movie before going to bed. But something was very wrong, and there would be no chilling or movie-watching tonight. Of that, he was certain.

Nina walked into the middle of the living room and stood beside the coffee table between the two sofas. "Can you explain these?"

His heart sank when he saw the photos. They were all of him and Chelsea. He picked up a picture that showed Chelsea straddling him in the back seat of the car he hired to take her back to the hotel. Every image looked damning, efficiently misrepresenting the nature of their contact.

"Nothing to say about photos that indicate you were nowhere near Ella's house on Friday night?" Nina asked. She spoke in a robotic voice, eyes devoid of emotion.

"Where did you get these? Were you having me followed?" He couldn't believe Nina would do something so sneaky.

"Not me. My mother." No warmth or welcome in her face or body, and her cold rejection chilled him to the bone.

"Why was Gloria having me followed?" he demanded. Nina's mother had never liked him, unfairly extending her disdain and anger about what his uncle had done to her, to his entire family.

"Obviously, she had good reason," Nina said.

"I know how these photos look, but they don't tell the whole story."

Nina folded her arms over her chest. "And what exactly is the whole story, Reese?"

He clearly had some work to do. If the roles were reversed, he would also have a hard time believing those photos represented a big misunderstanding.

"First of all, the photos are misleading. Chelsea was drunk, and all I did was make sure she got back to her hotel safely. That's it."

"Why a hotel?"

"She just moved here from New York."

"Who is she, and what is she to you? I've never heard you mention her name."

"I met her since you've been overseas. We met at Lindsay's book launch in New York a while back. She's a friend. I was simply helping her," Reese insisted.

"Only a friend? You haven't slept with her?"

He wanted to lie. He desperately wanted to lie, and somewhat dig out of the hole that had opened unexpectedly.

"Have you slept with her?" Nina demanded, the anger in her voice marred by hurt.

"Yes," Reese answered.

"When?"

"It's not important."

"Tell me when," she insisted. The fierce expression on her face left no room for dodging her questions.

"The last time was the weekend you returned to town. She was one of the women I spent the night with at the Ritz."

Nina laughed mirthlessly and propped her hands on her hips. "I see. *One* of the women. Okay, so, you were helping your buddy, your pal, someone who you've slept with as recently as three months ago, get back to her hotel because she was drunk. Do I have that right? Were you helping her in the back seat of the car, too, while she was on top of you? By the way, that looks very familiar. You do your best work in the back seat of cars."

"Stop it," Reese said, his voice a low snarl. "She was drunk and got a little handsy, but nothing happened between us."

"And still you went upstairs with her."

"To make sure she got back to her room safely. It was the decent thing to do."

"What a Good Samaritan you are," Nina said derisively.

"Nothing happened!"

"If nothing happened, why didn't you tell me about her instead of lying to me?"

"I didn't lie..."

She arched a brow when his words trailed off. "Is it coming back to you now? The same night you saw Chelsea was the same night you told me you went to Ella's, and you came back late and went right into the shower. I asked you about your visit to Ella when you came in. I asked about the wet spot on your pants."

Reese wasn't guilty of wrongdoing, but sweat trickled down his spine. "I went right into the shower because she'd thrown up on me."

Chelsea threw up on him in the car. After putting her to bed, he cleaned as much of the vomit off his slacks as he could and then left, anxious to get home and out of the filthy clothes.

"Did you at any point go over to Ella's on Friday night?"

This couldn't be happening. He'd spent the past week and a half thoroughly enjoying the woman he loved, living a dream, and now everything was falling apart. "The answer is complicated and can't be answered with a simple yes or no."

"Did you, or did you not spend the evening with your nieces getting sweaty because you were playing with them and their dog?" She spoke louder, in a voice filled with accusation.

"I have a good reason for doing what I did."

"Did you, or did you not lie to me about where you were going and what you did?"

Reese swallowed hard and realized that the surprise

proposal he had been planning would have to be squashed in favor of the truth, or there would be no proposal—surprise or otherwise.

"You're right, I didn't go to Ella's house, but what you see in those pictures isn't the whole story. You want to know what I was doing Friday night? I went to get you an engagement ring. It was going to be a surprise."

"So, I'm supposed to believe you went to buy an engagement ring and then hooked up with Chelsea right after?"

"I didn't hook up with Chelsea," Reese grated. "We ran into each other outside of the jewelry store. If your mother was having me followed, then they must have captured where I went before that photo with Chelsea and me on the sidewalk. I was at Klopard Jewelers."

"If that's the case, where's the ring?" She mocked him by looking around the room as if the ring would suddenly appear on a side table or under some other piece of furniture. "Where is it?"

His jaw clenched in frustration. "I'm having it designed."

"*Ohhhh*, it's being designed so you can't show me the ring you went to purchase for my engagement, on the night you said you went to Ella's house, but got caught making out with a woman named Chelsea in the back of a car. Did I get all of that right?"

"I'm not lying!" Reese yelled.

"I don't believe you!" Nina yelled back. "Why did I bother to try with you? I should have known we wouldn't last. We're no good together."

"That's not true. We *have* been good together for the past ten days."

"And now our time is up. I want you to go. Get out of my house!" She shook with rage.

"I'm not going anywhere. Not until we get this straightened out."

"There is nothing to get straightened out. You and I are finished."

"Like hell we are. I know you love me, and I love you, and you know I love you. I told you. I've shown you."

"You know who has shown me that he loves me? Andy." She shot his name at Reese like an armor-piercing bullet.

His neck muscles tightened. "Don't mention him in the middle of this goddamn conversation."

"Why not? You might as well know the truth."

"What truth, Nina?"

Her bottom lip trembled. "Andy and I were on a temporary break."

He couldn't make sense of the words she spoke. Her answer shook him to the core. "What did you say?"

"We were on a break. Thank you for the fun times and the great sex, but I'm going back to a man who wouldn't cheat on me. Who has patiently waited for me to get my shit together. I'm going back to the man who has the same dreams and aspirations as I do and wants the same life as I do. I'm going back to Andy."

"No, you're not."

"Yes, I am."

"Then what have we been doing for the past ten days?" he yelled.

"Filling time."

He thought back to the first night he saw her at the ice cream parlor. She'd said they had an argument, and he'd been gleeful that they had problems and wanted to make the forlorn look in her eyes disappear. "What?" he whispered.

"You heard me."

Reese charged over to where she stood and grabbed her shoulders. Her eyes widened, but she stared defiantly back at him. "Don't do this, Nina. Don't make me beg."

"I don't want you to beg. I want you to let go."

He rested his forehead against hers. "I can't. I can't, I *can't.*" He squeezed harder than he should, but he literally couldn't let go.

"Let me go, Reese. If you don't leave now, I'm going to call security."

"I wouldn't do this. You know me," he whispered shakily.

"No, I don't," she replied. Sorrow thickened her voice. "I saw what I wanted to see."

Reese's hands and shoulders dropped in defeat. He couldn't do this anymore. He kept chasing Nina, but she'd shown him in so many ways that his feelings weren't reciprocated. The other night he told her that he loved her, and she hadn't said a word, and yet he believed—held out hope—that what he saw in her eyes was love, too. When in reality, she didn't want him. In reality, she and Andy were going to be together, and he was just a *filler.* He was her placeholder, the way other women were his placeholder for her.

"You got me," he whispered. Pain, loss, and regret—his constant companions—had once again reared their ugly heads and ensnared him. "You got me good. I guess we both see what we want to see because I'm the idiot trying to make you into the woman *I* want you to be, because I love you so much. But you keep showing me that I don't mean shit to you."

He laughed shortly, with biting bitterness that did little to convey the true depth of his despair. "I was almost a father, and you kept that from me. After three years, you show up with Andy and then put his ring on your finger, when you know I want to be with you, and you kiss me the same way I kiss you— like you'll never get enough. The past ten days, you led me to believe that you and I were starting over, and you really wanted to be with me, but it was all a lie. Those photos gave you the excuse you needed to walk away." He swallowed hard. "I don't know you either, Nina. But what I do know is that I'm done. I'm not begging you. I'm not chasing you anymore. I guess whatever

Andy offers—whatever dreams you share—are enough. You want to be with him, go for it. You and I never have to speak again."

Reese turned on his heels and left the apartment. He wasn't just leaving Nina behind. He was also leaving his heart—stomped to pieces—behind, too.

CHAPTER 28

"No. I don't like it."

Nina wearily dropped her arms to her sides when Gloria voiced her displeasure yet again.

She officially hated wedding dress shopping. She'd spent the past couple of days trying on dress after dress, and her mother's constant negativity was stressing her out. She couldn't wait for this process to be over.

This one happened to be her favorite because it fit her style and personality. The lace caftan dress was made of a comfortable and light flowy fabric. She liked the design and fit so much, she didn't see a need to alter a single part of the garment.

She turned to Lindsay, pleading for help with her eyes. Her sister sat on the rose-gold sofa accented with mahogany wood. It matched the rest of the private dressing room, decorated in traditional furnishings and textured wallpaper in cream and rose-gold. Gloria sat perched on a burgundy armchair far away from her oldest daughter.

Their coolness toward each other was the other part of the process that drained Nina. There were better ways to spend the day than with her mother and her sister, both of whom could not get along. She couldn't really blame Lindsay because their mother treated Lindsay differently than she did Nina. Nina's father was Gloria's second husband and had been a millionaire. Lindsay's father had done a lot of terrible things and hurt people when he was alive.

"What do you think?" Nina asked her sister, fanning out the skirt with her hands. She really loved this dress.

"Cute, but not my personal taste. You know I like flashy, but you have to get what *you* want." Lindsay's very pointed words made their mother's lips flatten with displeasure.

"It's so plain," Gloria said, wincing as if the unattractiveness of the dress pained her. She stepped onto the raised platform and met Nina's eyes in the mirror. "Try something else. I want to see what a more traditional dress would look like on you."

Knowing her mother, she wanted Nina to try another dress not only because she didn't like the design of this one, but because she wanted a famous name on the label so she could brag to her friends. She'd urged Nina to commission a custom-made dress from Vera Wang or some other well-known designer, but taking one off the rack was Nina's own small act of defiance.

"We have several I can pull for you," said the saleswoman Elizabeth, who was also the assistant manager.

Nina had forgotten she was in the room. She stood quietly off to the side, hands clasped in front of her, a long dark braid hanging over one shoulder.

Nina's jaw tightened. She could barely look at Elizabeth because of the freckles across her pale nose. The minute she stepped on the sales floor and saw the woman, her mind flooded with memories of kissing Reese's freckled nose or the freckles on his shoulders.

The past couple of weeks, she couldn't bear to hear his name. It hurt so much, and the pain settled deep, deep in her chest. Thoughts of him and Chelsea and their big fight tormented her.

I'm not chasing you anymore.

"Bring me what you have. Three options, please." She studied her reflection and smoothed a hand over the fabric. What did it matter if she didn't get to wear this dress? One more compromise wouldn't hurt. The ceremony was only one day in the rest of her life.

The assistant manager left, and Nina disappeared into the fitting room to undress and wait. She hung up the dress and fondly swiped her hand down the front one more time.

The light on her phone flashed, which indicated she had missed a call. There was a text message from Andy.

Andy: Thinking about you. How is everything going?

Nina: I need a drink. Don't be surprised if I order a stiff one at dinner tonight.

Andy: About that, I have to cancel. My father wants me to attend another networking thing tonight in New York, so I'm flying out this afternoon. Be back Monday.

Disappointed, Nina sat down on the cushioned bench. Since getting back together, they'd picked a wedding date at the end of the month. *Let's get married. Let's not wait,* he'd said. In two more weeks, she'd become Nina von Trapp, and she wondered if he could manage to make time for them to go on their honeymoon.

Nina: Wish you didn't have to go. Call me when you get there.

Andy: I will. Love you.

She stared at the words. They may not have passion, but he was safe. Security before passion.

I'm done. I'm not chasing you anymore.

Nina: Love you, too.

She didn't have time to dwell too long on her thoughts because the saleswoman returned with three dresses and hung them on the rack. She helped Nina into the first one with a corset-designed bodice that squeezed her torso and made her stand up straighter.

"Do you like it?" Elizabeth walked in a circle around her, adjusting here and there.

"It's fine."

"You should love your dress."

Nina met her gaze in the mirror and smiled faintly. "It's only one day. Let's see what my mother and sister think."

They thought it was good, but not great. She tried on the next one, which also met with a tepid response, though her mother was much more enthusiastic about these gowns than the previous ones Nina had chosen.

When she donned the last dress and stepped out of the fitting room and onto the raised platform, her mother gasped.

Lindsay's mouth hung open. "Wow," her sister said.

Elizabeth crouched before her and fluffed the skirt, and Gloria slowly approached with tear-filled eyes. She stepped up beside Nina. "This is it. You truly look like a bride."

The dress was extravagant, over-the-top, and absolutely not what she came here to buy, but the expression on her family's faces made it the perfect purchase. The dress sparkled, with an off-the-shoulder neckline and a fitted bodice covered in rhinestones. The voluminous skirt combined layers of tulle and satin that visually had an ethereal effect and made her look like a princess.

"I do look like a bride." Nina turned her back to the mirror and examined the rear view over her shoulder.

"Are you ready for the veil?" Elizabeth asked.

Nina nodded, and Elizabeth fitted the tiara and veil onto her head.

"You look stunning," the assistant manager said.

"Andy is going to fall in love with you all over again when he sees you. This is it. Don't you think this is it?" her mother asked anxiously, eyes still filled with tears.

Yes, she looked like a bride. Yes, the dress was beautiful, but it wasn't what she wanted. But sometimes, sacrifices had to be made. Compromises reached. It might not be her dream gown, but it was good enough.

In a short while, she would walk down the aisle and say *I do*. Emotion clogged her throat, tying up the words she needed to say. Was it excitement, nervousness, or something else? Whatever it was, she managed to push through and answer her mother.

"Yes, this is it," Nina said.

CHAPTER 29

a sharp knock sounded on the bedroom door. Then it eased open.

"Reese, you have a guest," Javier said.

"I don't want to talk to anyone." The pillows over his head muffled the words.

Last night Reese went drinking with two friends. People with no job and few responsibilities had no qualms about drinking on a weeknight, but he knew better. Long after they left, he stayed at the bar and downed more liquor, going so far as to buy several rounds for the people seated around him so he wouldn't have to drink alone. But the pain of losing Nina couldn't be diminished by alcohol.

He only made himself miserable. Right now, he lay sprawled across the bed on his stomach with the sheets tangled around his legs and a splitting headache. He'd slept all day off and on, and in general, felt like crap.

"He said you would want to talk to him. His name is Andy von Trapp."

Andy von Trapp?

Reese lifted his head from beneath the pillows and squinted

against the light coming in the door behind his housekeeper. "What does he want?"

"He didn't say, except that he wanted to talk to you about something personal."

There was nothing he wanted to talk to Andy about unless he wanted to tell Reese that he was going to disappear off the face of the planet. Reese would gladly talk to him about that.

"Should I ask him to leave?"

Curiosity got the better of him, and Reese sat up. "No. Give me a few minutes to wash my face, and I'll come out."

Javier nodded and closed the door behind him.

What did Andy want? *Guess I'll have to find out*, Reese thought.

He threw off the covers and stumbled into the bathroom. He looked a little bleary-eyed, but not too bad, considering the night he had. He brushed his teeth and washed his face, and then pulled on a pair of jeans. He didn't bother with a shirt. This was his house, and Andy had arrived uninvited and without warning, so he'd have to deal with Reese's naked torso.

He walked into the living room, and Andy rose from the sofa. He looked well put together, his dark hair slicked down on one side, and wearing a tailored charcoal suit and red tie.

He looked at Reese's naked chest and raised an eyebrow. "Did I interrupt something?"

"I was taking a nap."

"Long night?"

"Let's skip the chitchat. We're not friends. Why are you here?"

Andy smiled faintly. "To talk, man-to-man."

Man-to-man was never a good phrase and always meant trouble, but Reese was in a trouble-making mood. Here stood the person who had taken away the love of his life. Maybe he'd take advantage of this opportunity to tell Andy a few words himself, man-to-man.

"About what?"

Andy stuck one hand in his jacket pocket. "About *whom*."

His eyes followed Andy as he ambled around the living room, gaze touching on various pieces of furniture and the decorative items on the walls, as if checking out the place to buy it.

"I remembered you from Westerly Academy." He swiveled to face Reese.

"So, you lied."

He shrugged. "Having a little fun. Bothered you, didn't it? That I couldn't remember who you were."

What the heck was going on? He didn't know why Andy was there or what direction the conversation was going in, but he was already tired of it and not in the mood for any foolishness.

"I couldn't care less, to be honest. I barely remember that afternoon." Reese affected a bored voice, but he remembered every detail of that afternoon—at least the portions that included Nina. He remembered the yellow and white dress she wore, her straightened hair framing her face, and the devastating news that she had accepted Andy's proposal.

One of the worst days of his life, second only to the moment when he walked out of her apartment for good a couple of weeks ago.

"You and your buddies thought you were so cool in school, running around like top dogs. You, Mister Popular, the leader of the pack. I couldn't stand you and your crew."

"We never bothered you. We never even talked to you."

"You didn't have to. You talked about me. Called me Saint Andy because I didn't participate in your wild escapades or find your behavior remotely attractive."

That part was true, but those comments had been between Reese and his closest friends. Apparently, Andy had found out.

"I'm not going back down memory lane with you, talking

about stuff that happened when we were kids. What do you want?"

"I want you to know the truth about me and Nina. I saw her once at a charity function. I did a little research and found out she was the daughter of Tyrus Winthrop of The Winthrop Hotel Group, who'd passed away. Our business interests aligned perfectly, and she had poise and class—the kind of woman a man like me wants to have by his side. My mother happened to know her mother because they occasionally saw each other at the spa. A few weeks later, she became a little more friendly with Gloria during her weekly spa visit, and they hit it off. It seemed like everything was aligning for me to be in her life, but then she abruptly left the country, and I didn't know what to do. Until, with a little help, I decided to be the man she wanted."

Reese couldn't believe what he heard. "You sneaky little shit. You didn't happen to run into her in New Zealand. You planned the whole encounter."

A self-satisfied smirk tugged up the corners of Andy's mouth. "Damn right, and don't bother thinking you have to tell Nina. She knows and forgave me after she took a little break to clear her head."

Reese laughed softly and folded his arms over his chest. "Oh, so that's what the break was about?"

"She and I are good now."

"If you're so good, why are you here?"

"Because I know the two of you have history and saw the way you looked at her at Richard and Ingela's engagement party. I also learned that the two of you spent time together during our brief separation." His face hardened into unpleasant lines. "I'm here to warn you. I don't need you confusing her. She chose me, Brooks, so if you'd kindly stay the hell away from her, I'd appreciate it."

"Or what? You won't do a damn thing." Reese cocked his head to the side and challenged Andy with his eyes. "Did Nina tell you what she did on her break, while she and I were spending time together? Did she mention that I fucked her every night for six nights straight? Sometimes in the daytime, too. No?"

He took great pleasure in watching Andy's face pale and his smirk disappear.

"Guess she needed a little excitement before she got tied down. Better bring your A-game, bruh, because if I catch you slipping in the future, I'll fuck her again—give her more of that excitement she can't get with your saintly ass. Fuck outta here." He dismissed Andy with a curt, backhanded wave.

Two spots of red color inflamed Andy's cheeks. He swung a right hook, but Reese stepped back and easily dodged the blow because he'd anticipated it.

"You only get one," he warned, holding up a finger.

Andy raised his fist again, trembling with rage. "You son of a—"

Reese stepped into his face. "Say one word about my mother, and you'll be eating my knuckles. Get out of here, and don't ever step to me again."

Both men glared at each other, only inches apart. Then Andy let out a disdainful, nasty chuckle.

"I feel sorry for you. You love her, don't you? You must, or you wouldn't keep hanging around, begging for her time, sleeping with her when you know she belongs to me. Makes you feel like shit, doesn't it? That no matter what you do, she'll never love you the way that you love her. That no matter how good you think you fucked her, she's wearing my ring and marrying me in one week." He whispered the next words. "You had her for six nights, but she's mine for the rest of our lives."

Reese swallowed back his hatred for the man before him. He hated him for no other reason than from now until death, he would be the one who kissed Nina. He would be the one she climbed into bed with each night, and he got to make love to her. She would kiss his shoulders when he was up late working and be the mother of his children. Be his partner, his confidante, his friend.

Andy snickered as he backed away. "Have a nice life."

He left Reese standing there, immobile after the door had closed, and he was all alone.

With a low growl, he punched the wall hard, imagining it was Andy's face. Cracks appeared in the sheetrock, but it didn't break. He slammed his fist two more times in the same space, and his fist cracked through on the third blow. He pulled back his hand and stared at the tiny cuts and his red knuckles.

Andy's words banged in his head like a relentless gong.

She's mine for the rest of our lives.

CHAPTER 30

*N*ina needed a break. Hands on her hips, she stretched her back and shoulder muscles to loosen the tightening caused by hours of work. Her assistant Craig continued to work diligently, sorting papers and files into five different boxes. Despite his tall, bulky frame, he moved quickly. Beads of perspiration dotted his brown skin, but he wouldn't slow down. Craig only knew two speeds—fast and faster.

Nina took a good look around her father's old study. His favorite sweatshirt from his alma mater—Howard University—hung over the back of the leather sofa, and there were albums filled with photos—mostly of her—because Tyrus Winthrop had considered himself an amateur photographer. What better subject than his own daughter to capture on film?

Now that she was the CEO of The Winthrop Hotel Group, she needed a decent home office and decided to take over this space, since Andy planned to give up his apartment and move into hers. She and her assistant spent the morning going over ideas for the redesign and then started on the papers in the desk and file cabinet.

Her father had been an avid reader, mostly thrillers and

mysteries. The bookshelves lining the walls were filled with his favorite authors in the genre. Some days, he sat in here, feet propped on the desk, body angled to the small window that looked out over the rooftops of nearby buildings as he indulged in his favorite pastime for an hour or two.

She intended to donate many of the books but keep the special editions and signed copies. In the empty spaces, she intended to place knickknacks and mementos from her travels, surrounding herself with positive energy and great memories.

Nina turned in a circle, already envisioning the changes that would transform this into a space she could call her own. She smiled slightly at an album she'd left open on the desk the last time she'd been in here. She gazed down at her father's smiling face. She was about nine in the photo, standing in front of him, holding up a certificate for winning the class spelling bee. His hand rested on her shoulder, and he beamed proudly as if she'd received the Nobel Prize for Literature.

She should enlarge the image and hang it on the wall in a nice frame. It was one of her favorites of her and her dad.

"Miss you, Daddy," Nina whispered. In a few days, she was getting married, and he wouldn't be there to walk her down the aisle. She would walk herself down the aisle, a decision she made that annoyed her mother, but Nina refused to budge. If her father couldn't escort her down the aisle, she didn't want anyone else.

"This looks valuable. Found it in the back of that closet." Craig showed her an opened jewelry box. The only thing inside was an envelope and a necklace with a large ruby pendant with diamond pieces designed to cover one half of the huge stone.

Choking on a sudden flood of emotion, Nina took the box. "This was a college graduation gift."

"From your dad?"

She swallowed. "No. From Reese. The necklace belonged to his grandmother," she whispered.

The first time she saw the necklace had been one night when they were lying next to each other on his bed, and she watched him scroll through photos and tell her about his most recent trip to Brazil, where his paternal grandmother was from. That's when she saw the enormous stone in the middle of Reese's palm. He showed it off to the camera. His grandmother had left it for him when she passed.

Nina had fallen in love with it right away.

"It's vintage," Reese explained. "Her mother gave it to her, and she wore it on her wedding day when she married my grandfather."

"It's gorgeous." Nina traced a hand over the photo as if she could touch it.

"You like it?"

"I love it, but I like old jewelry." She shrugged, unable to take her eyes from the photo.

"I'll give it to you."

She looked at him in shock. "What? No."

"I mean it. It's yours if you want it."

"Really?" she asked, breathless with anticipation.

"Not right now. You can get it as a graduation present when we finish college. Assuming you're good and stay with me."

"Reese, that's four years away!"

"You want the necklace or not?" he asked.

"Ooh, you make me sick!" She playfully pouted. "You promise you'll give it to me?"

"Promise."

"Fine. I'll stay with you then."

He gave an evil villain laugh. "My devilish plan has worked."

"Only because I want that necklace."

He turned onto his side, giving her his undivided attention. "That's the only reason?"

"No," she said softly.

Reese pulled her on top of him. "Then, why?"

"You know why." She lowered her gaze and pressed her finger to the pulse at the base of his throat.

"Tell me," he prodded gently.

"You're going to make me say it?" she asked shyly. Expressing her feelings for him was still so new.

"You know I like to hear it."

She sighed dramatically. "Because I love you."

"Because what?" Reese cupped one ear.

She giggled. "Because I love you."

She kissed him then because she couldn't help herself. He was adorable and sweet, and she felt like the luckiest person in the world. He didn't have to bribe her. She would stay with him as long as he wanted her.

"Love you, too, baby. Love you so damn much." He rolled her onto her back.

With a heavy heart, Nina pulled the handwritten note from the envelope. Reese had terrible penmanship, and she used to tease him and say he could write prescriptions. Nonetheless, she understood every word he wrote.

I remember how much you loved the necklace, and I promised it to you. It's not your fault we're not together. Enjoy it.

She couldn't believe he'd remembered that she'd liked it and intended to keep his promise, even though they were no longer a couple. She tried to give it back and included a note of thanks, but he returned everything to her by courier.

Exasperated, she went to see him in person and thrust the jewelry box at him. "I can't accept this."

Reese stood there, with his arms folded, glaring at her as if she were trying to steal the necklace instead of giving it back.

"I'm not taking it back."

"Then I'll ship it to you."

"And I'll ship it right back."

"Why are you—"

"Nina, just take it. I want you to have it. I need to know you have it."

They both looked at each other for a spell, their shared pain laid open and exposed for each other to see.

She ducked her head to hide the tears that sprang to her eyes. He probably saw them, but she kept her eyes trained on the ground anyway, hiding how much it had hurt to let him go.

"Okay. Thank you."

She couldn't hide the thickened, trembling tone of her voice. She quickly turned and left.

They never spoke about the necklace again.

REESE IGNORED THE RINGING PHONE.

He didn't want to talk to anyone. Matter of fact, he seriously considered going somewhere alone for a few days so he wouldn't have to speak to a soul or answer questions about how he was feeling because he and Nina had split. He knew his family meant well, but they were driving him crazy with their concern. The way they acted, you'd think he was a terminal cancer patient.

He pressed the button on the remote continuously. The screen flickered as he mindlessly ran through the channels, searching for a movie or show to hold his interest.

Pounding on the door made him jump. Who the heck could that be? After Andy's visit last week, he wasn't in the mood for any more unexpected visitors.

The knocking stopped, then started seconds later. Stopped and then started right back up again. Irritated, Reese pressed the power button, and the television screen went black.

He jumped up from the sofa and marched over to the door. Through the peephole, he saw his brother standing outside. *Shit.*

Stephan brought his eye close to the hole. "Open the door, Reese. I know you're in there."

Sighing, he reluctantly swung open the door and walked away.

Stephan followed him into the living room and watched as Reese collapsed onto the sofa and dropped his head back.

"You look like shit."

"Yeah, well, I feel like it, too. So I guess my appearance matches how I feel. What are you doing here? Unless you brought some weed, I don't need you in my apartment." He'd asked Stephan before, but his brother had refused. Today was the day—Nina's wedding day—and he didn't want to feel anything.

"You don't smoke weed. You smoked one time and hated it," Stephan reminded him.

"I want some. Are you going to get me some or not?"

"Not. I don't smoke anymore."

"Fine. I'll find someone who can get me what I want." Reese staggered up, but Stephan shoved him back down.

"Get off me, man!"

"That isn't the answer."

"Yes, it is! I don't want to feel anything." His voice cracked. Embarrassed, he buried his face in his hands. He shouldn't have opened the door. "Get the fuck out."

"There'll be someone else."

"I only want her."

Stephan dropped onto the cushion beside him. Two minutes passed before he spoke. "I'm not going to the wedding."

Reese lifted his head. "Why not? She's your friend."

"Mother told us not to, but even if she hadn't, I wouldn't have gone."

"You have no reason not to go. She didn't do anything to you."

Stephan shifted his eyes to Reese. "I can't go to that church and celebrate her marriage to a man who's not my brother, knowing how you feel about her. It wouldn't be right. My loyalty is to you."

Reese stared out the window. The gray, overcast sky fit his somber mood. "What about Ella and Simone?"

"They're not going, either. None of us are. Well, except Malik, because he's Lindsay's date."

He appreciated his family's support, but it still saddened him.

"You should go get her," Stephan said.

"Like it's that easy."

"It could be."

"So I should just forget the part where she's getting married today? Pretend she didn't choose Andy over me?" Reese shot his brother a questioning but irate look.

Stephan fell silent. After a while, he looked at Reese as if he'd just cracked the code to happiness. "Look, if you love Nina even half as much as I love Roselle, it's not too late. If you love her like you say you do, then do whatever you can to win her back. Climb mountains. Walk on hot coals. Run through fire, if you have to. The way I look at it, until she says 'I do,' you still have a shot."

* * *

LONG AFTER STEPHAN LEFT, Reese pondered his brother's words.

Since he couldn't dull his senses with drugs, he worked his way through a collector's edition of Patrón that he should have saved for a special occasion. There were only five hundred in the world, and after finishing the first one earlier this week, he was on his second bottle.

In the kitchen, he made another batanga with extra tequila and dragged himself into the living room. He felt a buzz coming on, which was perfect. Maybe he would be passed out soon and sleep through the afternoon.

He'd done his best not to think about her and their last argument, but with her wedding taking place in less than an hour, he couldn't do anything but think about her and their angry words to each other. He remembered the good times, too, like the cute way she put her foot down and protected him because of his allergy to strawberries. Or the way she lured him in with her sexy dancing at the club, and the rushed, hungry way they made love in the back of his Mercedes after so many years.

"Nina," he whispered, dropping his head back and closing his eyes. If Gloria hadn't had him followed and shown Nina those photos, she'd be wearing his ring now and planning to marry him. Then they'd be making plans to start a family and—

Wait a minute...

Reese's eyes flew open. There were two very definitive things he knew about Nina. She wanted to save the world, and she wanted to get married and have kids.

He sat up. *Was that it?*

He told her that he loved her but never said he wanted to get married and have children. Was that what she meant when she said Andy wanted the same life she did? Reese wanted all of those things, too—because of her. *With her.*

He scrambled to his feet. He needed to shower and change.

He had a wedding to stop.

CHAPTER 31

*A*lone in the dressing room, Nina added a little more pomade to the left side of her hair, which she had decided not to straighten as Andy had requested.

Something old.

Something new.

Something borrowed.

Something blue.

She removed Reese's grandmother's pendant from its chain and slipped it between her ample breasts. Her something old. She took a deep breath and closed her eyes. She still felt nauseous, but the glass of ginger ale calmed the queasiness. *Wedding day jitters*, her mother had said.

Raised voices came from inside the main suite, and Nina recognized the voices of her mother and sister. She rushed into the room. "What is going on? Could you two be nice to each other for one freaking day?"

If Lindsay's hazel-eyed glare could pierce their mother's flesh, she would do it. "Are you going to tell her, or should I?" Lindsay asked.

"Lindsay, don't do this." Gloria appeared angry, but a bit of fear manifested in her eyes and the tremor of her voice.

"*Tell her.*"

"Tell me what?" Nina looked between them. What could possibly be so terrible that her mother wouldn't want to tell her, and Lindsay would insist that she should?

"All right, since you won't tell her, I will. Our mother has entered into an arrangement with Corbin von Trapp. I overheard her talking to him. In exchange for convincing you to marry Andy, she gets a nice signing bonus of five million dollars and a regular allowance. Essentially, you're about to enter into an arranged marriage but didn't know it, orchestrated by Corbin and Gloria to merge the two businesses—The Winthrop Hotel Group and Von Trapp & Morrison, Inc."

Appalled, Nina looked at her mother. "Is that true?" She didn't need a reply, because her mother's expression answered the question.

"Yes," Gloria said.

"Does Andy know?"

"No. The...financial arrangement was strictly between me and his father."

"How could you do this to me? When is enough, enough for you?" Nina asked.

"Honey, I love you and want the best for you. I just happened to get a little something in the process."

"You are unbelievable," Lindsay said.

"You love yourself, Mom. You love money."

Lindsay had warned her plenty of times, but Nina ignored her sister's words because their relationship had been strained for years, and she assumed that the animosity between them skewed Lindsay's opinion of Gloria.

"What are you going to do?" Gloria actually looked frightened, probably because she feared losing out on the deal she'd made with Corbin. "Nina..."

"Don't talk to me right now," Nina snapped. "I need you to leave."

Gloria straightened as if someone had shoved a steel rod up her spine. "I will, but allow me to say one last thing. There are a lot of people out there on those pews—important people who came to see this wedding. Some of them have come from a very long way. Lots of money was spent, so to back out now because of a private arrangement that really should not change your decision to marry Andy would be foolhardy. Think about what you're doing. Who you are. Who you are marrying. Don't make a hasty, emotional decision. You can have a very happy life with Andy. Everything I've ever told you remains the same. Love is a fallacy. I'm not wrong."

"What are you talking about?" Lindsay interjected.

"You can have security. Respect. You'll have all of that with Andy. Those are the bricks to build your relationship on. Not passion. It's fleeting. It doesn't last. When you're old and gray, you won't feel that, but you'll have the security and respect of your partner. Andy is a good man, and he loves you. And more than anything, your father would have approved of him."

"How. Dare. You. Don't mention my father in your ridiculous effort to coerce me into doing what you want, Mom." This entire ordeal had stressed her out. "I want you to leave now, please."

"Make the right decision, Nina." After a murderous glance at Lindsay, Gloria walked out.

"Unbelievable." Lindsay rested a hand on her shoulder. "Are you okay?"

Nina let out a shaky laugh. "No."

"I'm sorry this happened to you."

"Two hundred people are waiting out there for us," Nina said quietly.

"Let them wait. Take your time and make the decision that's

right for you." That advice sounded similar to the advice she'd received from Sylvie Johnson.

"I need to be alone."

"Okay." Lindsay gave her a hug and then left.

Nina sat down in an armchair and closed her eyes.

* * *

THE CHURCH DOORS OPENED, and the organist began the timeless, familiar song that millions of brides had marched to. Wagner's "Bridal Chorus" filled the church as Nina walked alone down the aisle with an ivory bouquet toward the minister and her future husband and their bridal party of six. She passed by friends and acquaintances, family members, business associates, everyone smiling and excited for her on her big day.

When she arrived at the end of the longest walk of her life, Andy helped her up the three steps to stand beside him. He lifted her veil, and they smiled at each other. After a few words by the officiant, the ceremony began in earnest.

Nina slid a glance at Andy from the corner of her eye. He looked so confident about this major step when inside she quivered with uncertainty. Terror. That was the only way to describe her racing heart and the fear that gripped her at the thought of spending the rest of her life with the man beside her. Instead of diminishing, the fear expanded and multiplied. This feeling was way worse than wedding jitters.

He'd been so understanding about her sexual reconnection with Reese. A little angry at first, which was to be expected, but he'd had no problem moving forward with the wedding. She hadn't been so understanding when Reese slept with Kelly. She'd been devastated and wanted nothing to do with him. How could Andy have taken it so well? Did he love her that much?

Oh, my god.

He hadn't easily moved forward with the wedding because he loved her. He found it easy to do because he *didn't* love her.

She looked at him again—really looked at him. The rigid profile and firm set to his jaw indicated a man of strength. A man of determination. A man to be respected. A safe man. But not a man in love.

He turned his head toward her. Coming out of her own thoughts, she noticed an awkward tension in the air. Everyone was looking at her. They waited for a response.

The minister cleared his throat and repeated the vows. "I, Nina Winthrop, take you, Andy von Trapp, for my lawful husband, to have and to hold from this day forward."

She didn't want to embarrass him or his family, but she didn't want a marriage of convenience. She didn't want safe. She wanted a marriage filled with love, passion, excitement, and all its iterations.

Andy's face remained stoic, but panic filled his eyes. "It's okay, honey. I know you're nervous, but you have to say the words." He let out a strained laugh.

"Andy..." What could she possibly say at this moment?

The doors at the back of the church burst open. All eyes swung in that direction. Reese stumbled through wearing a cream suit and a darker tie.

"Nina!" he bellowed, as two well-dressed members of the security team—one Black and the other white—tackled him to the carpet.

Gasps filled the church at the unfolding spectacle.

"Ninaaaaa!" Her name sounded like a hoarse, desperate plea. "Don't marry him! I love you! Don't marry him!"

Twisting like a snake, he slipped out of his jacket and left it behind in one of the security guys' hands.

Reese rushed toward her, but the white male moved fast and grabbed him in a headlock, then the other security guard lifted his feet off the floor. Obstinately, he continued to wriggle in desperation as they fought to remove him from the building.

"Nina!"

Don't hurt him, she thought, taking a step forward and reaching out a hand as if she could save him from that distance.

Andy grabbed her arm. "What are you doing?" he asked, looking horrified.

"Hey!" Malik yelled. Big, brawny, and bearded, he looked like a member of security himself. He elbowed his way through his pew to the aisle. He grabbed the Black security guard from behind in a bear hug and wrestled him away from Reese.

"Nina, marry me instead!" Reese yelled, as security dragged him backward, kicking and wrestling to break free.

"Wait!" Nina yelled out in a shaky voice.

All eyes shifted from the back to the front, and the entire sanctuary fell quiet.

The white security guard relaxed his hold on Reese, and Malik released the Black guy. Like everyone else in the church, they were transfixed by what was playing out before them.

Breathing heavily from the exertion, Reese took one step forward. "I want the same life you do. Be my wife, and let's have a bunch of babies together."

His voice filled the church with the most beautiful words Nina had ever heard. Happiness overflowed in her chest.

"I only want three," she said, daring to smile, daring to believe.

"Then we'll have three."

"Nina, what are you doing?" Andy asked in a hushed voice. Two spots of color darkened his cheeks.

"I'm sorry," she said in a soft voice. She looked at Reese. "Yes, I'll marry you!"

More gasps and whispers erupted in the church.

Nina handed off the bouquet to her sister, who grinned ear to ear. Heart racing, she gathered her skirt and hurried down the stairs. She ran past the front row and her mother's stricken face and Corbin's open-mouthed fury. Past wide-eyed guests, half with their mouths hanging open and others whispering in shock.

Reese met her halfway and lifted her into his arms. They hugged each other tightly as if they would never let go. When he finally placed her back on her feet, he clutched her face and kissed her eyes, cheeks, and lips.

"I love you so damn much…" He was breathing hard after the struggle, but she heard every word as clearly as a bell. "If you told me I had to wait an eternity, I would. As long as I get to spend it with you."

"I promise you don't have to wait that long." Tears streamed down her face, and he swiped them away with his thumbs. "Enough time has passed. I love you, Reese. I love you." Her voice cracked, and more tears fell. Finally admitting the truth out loud was so freeing.

He kissed her again, gently. Her lips, her tear-soaked cheeks, as if they were the only ones in the building and didn't have an audience.

"Let's go," he said.

Hand in hand, they ran out of the church together.

ina floated across the floor of the luxury suite at the Wynn Hotel in Las Vegas with a fruity drink in hand.

She was still getting used to the fact that they'd gotten married only hours before, and she was now Reese's wife.

Nina Brooks.

Mrs. Nina Brooks.

Both sounded perfect.

Reese glanced up in the middle of sending a text. He sat beside the window in an oversized armchair, his eyes trained on her progress, a soft smile lifting his lips at the corners. He wore a pair of boxers and no shirt because she had taken his shirt to cover the white lacy thong she wore underneath. His grandmother's necklace and pendant hung around her neck, which she had worn during their Las Vegas ceremony.

"Try this." Nina extended the drink to Reese and straddled his thighs, folding her legs beneath her on either side of his knees.

"What is this?"

"Fruit juices with a splash of rum. My personal rum punch

recipe. It's a proprietary blend."

He lifted his eyebrows. "Proprietary, huh?" He took a sip.

"You like it?"

He grinned. "Anything you do, I like."

Smiling, she cupped his face and gave him a quick smooch. She'd been smiling a lot ever since they left the church and learned Reese had chartered a flight to Vegas.

They collected some very important items before they left Atlanta. They stopped by the wedding boutique so she could purchase the Bohemian dress with the kimono sleeves. Fortunately, it hadn't been sold. On the second stop, they picked up their rings from Klopard Jewelers.

Nina examined the big diamond on her finger.

"You keep looking at your rings. You don't like them?" Reese set the drink on the table beside the chair.

The main stone, round and the size of a boulder, lay nestled against the chevron-shaped, diamond-encrusted wedding band that also had one small diamond attached at the vee and two on either side. She adored the design, but...

"This diamond is...big," she said.

"You deserve it."

"The size doesn't have anything to do with Andy, does it?"

"Maybe a tiny bit."

"*Reese.*" She sighed.

"What's the problem?"

"I can't walk around with this thing on my finger."

"Why not?" He glared at her.

"I'll need armed guards with me at all times."

"Then we'll hire armed guards."

"Sweetheart, baby, you're being unreasonable. I have a great idea. How about we cut the diamond into two or three more pieces of jewelry? I can keep the ring but also get a necklace or two out of this."

Reese continued to glare at her.

"Shouldn't I get what *I* want?" She stared right back at him.

He let out a weary sigh. "All right. As long as the ring you end up wearing is bigger than Andy's."

"Oh my goodness, it doesn't matter!"

"It matters to me," he said, a stubborn set to his jaw.

She shook her head. Then she laughed softly, leaned in, and kissed him again. "Fine."

"Thank you." Reese cupped her bottom and pulled her snugly against his body, so their hips were aligned. "Did we just have our first fight as a married couple?"

"Not a fight, but definitely a disagreement, and we managed to resolve it quickly."

"I think we might be good at this marriage thing."

"I think so, too." She pressed another kiss to his lips, longer this time, tasting the fullness of his mouth and the sweetness of the rum punch.

Nina shifted positions and sat across his lap, her legs dangling over the arm of the chair and Reese's arms holding her close against his chest.

"Remember our conversation at Centennial Park?" he asked.

"Mmm-hmm." She felt safe and snug in his arms, without a single regret that she'd married him.

"You're my happy place."

Nina lifted her head to look at him.

His thumb gently stroked beneath her lower lip. "I'm content, happy, at peace whenever I'm with you. Wherever you are, that's where I want to be, and that's where I'll be happy."

"Reese…"

He kissed the bridge of her nose and her forehead. "I mean it. I love you so much. And I'm happiest when I'm with you. Always."

"You're my happy place, too. Just like this, in your arms. Love you," she said softly against his lips.

His hands lowered to her bottom and squeezed, and his

growing erection signaled that they'd soon have to move this conversation to the bedroom, but the phone rang and forestalled their movement.

Reese groaned, picked it up, and showed her the name on the screen. His brother Stephan. Reese had texted him earlier.

He answered the phone and put it on speaker. "Hello?"

"Have you lost all common sense? When I told you to go get her, I didn't mean marry her right now. You don't know if you can trust what she's feeling. She was about to marry another man, and you—"

"You're on speaker. And she's here."

Awkward silence. "Oh."

"Hi, Stephan." Earlier that day, she had been about to marry another man, and now here she was, married to Reese. Nina understood that Stephan was looking out for his brother, and she couldn't blame him for that.

"Hi, Nina," Stephan said cautiously. "Um, about what I said—"

"Thank you for telling him to come get me."

"Oh, yeah, of course. I knew he loved you, and you were made for each other." Stephan cleared his throat. "Have you told Mother? She's going to be upset that you ran off and got married without her knowledge."

"I sent a text to her and Father right before I sent one to you. I expect to hear from them any minute now. But she'll be happy. She's always loved Nina."

"Yeah, well, okay. I guess you know what you're doing."

"Yes, I do. Like you knew what you were doing when you married Roselle," Reese said pointedly.

Stephan and his wife had had the equivalent of a shotgun wedding earlier in the year.

Stephan laughed. "Point made. I'll see you when you get back."

"All right."

No sooner had he hung up, did the phone ring again. This time, his mother.

"Oh, boy." He braced himself for the call and put it on speaker, as well. "Hello, Mother."

Sylvie let out a heavy sigh, and Reese rolled his eyes as he prepared for the guilt trip. Nina covered her mouth to stifle a giggle.

"I don't know where I went wrong. Neither of my sons gave me a proper wedding. Both of them simply ran off and kept me from the pleasure of a ceremony. Fortunately, I have two daughters who were not so selfish."

"I'm sorry. We can have a celebration when Nina and I get back to Atlanta, the same way you did with Stephan and Roselle."

"It's not the same, but it will have to do, I suppose. Speaking of Nina, how is she?"

Reese nudged Nina.

"Hello! I'm right here, and as happy as can be," she said.

"Oh, hello, my darling!" Sylvie's voice changed, going from dramatic melancholy to excitement. "Welcome to the family. Welcome, welcome, welcome. We won't dwell on the past, but I'm quite happy that you and my son are together, the way I always thought you should be. And I even forgive you for not letting me have a wedding ceremony."

"Thank you." Trying hard not to laugh, Nina met Reese's eyes, and he shook his head at his mother's theatrics.

"You and I need to talk when you get back. The celebration can be as big or as small as you like, but I would recommend something in the early afternoon. Perhaps a nice luncheon with—"

"Sylvie, leave those kids alone so they can enjoy each other and have some privacy. You can make all your plans when they get back." Oscar's voice was weary but also contained a trace of amusement.

"Very well. Of course, you're right," Sylvie said. "Good night, my darlings."

"Good night, you two. Don't rush back," Oscar said. She heard the smile in her father-in-law's voice.

"Good night," Nina and Reese said in unison.

* * *

REESE LEANED back in the jetted tub. He laughed to himself as he relaxed in the warm, sudsy water that smelled like roses, which meant he would smell like roses. *Roses.* The things he'd do for this woman.

He touched the platinum wedding band on his finger. He was actually married and couldn't wait for all aspects of married life—sleeping together in the same bed every night, waking up next to each other in the morning, great sex, and together accomplishing goals that would benefit their future children.

Nina padded into the bathroom in a silk robe and an elastic band in her hand. Her bouncy, full natural hair fell around her ears in a messy array of curls, courtesy of their intense love-making earlier.

"Get in here, woman."

"I'm coming. Dang, you're so impatient."

Facing the mirror, Nina used the elastic band to pin her hair on top of her head in a fluffy ponytail, dropped the robe, and then climbed into the tub. Reese groaned as she settled her soft ass against him. Putting his arms around her, he brushed his nose along her nape and ear.

"What are you going to do about your mother?" he asked.

"I don't know yet. We have to talk, but our relationship is forever changed. I guess I should do like Lindsay and keep her at arm's length, but that's hard. She's my mother."

"Don't compromise to satisfy her or anyone else. Her toxicity is not your burden to bear."

Nina nodded her agreement but remained silent, swirling her fingers back and forth in the sudsy water. "I hope we always get along like this."

"All you have to do is remember I'm always right, so just agree with me. Happy spouse, happy house."

Nina laughed. "That's not how our marriage is going to work."

"No, seriously, when we argue, we'll work on getting back to this place. And just so you know, when you get tired of my ass, I'm not divorcing you. You're stuck with me."

She laughed again. "So, you're going to keep me tied to you whether or not I want to be?"

"That's right. Don't say I didn't warn you."

"There are millions of things worse than being tied to the love of my life forever."

Reese pressed a kiss to her temple. "I'm never letting you out of my sight again."

"I never want to be let out of your sight again." Nina turned her head and kissed him and then turned back around.

He was ridiculously content and felt invincible—like he could face any obstacle. His heart and soul were full.

"What do you want to do tomorrow?" Reese asked, looping an arm around her neck.

"Let's go see a show. Or…"

She went through a list of activities she wanted to do, which she'd obviously been contemplating. The sound of her voice soothed him. With the same arm, he squeezed her closer and pressed a kiss to the side of her neck.

Nina lightly elbowed him. "Quit and listen to what I'm saying."

Reese chuckled. "Mean ass. I'm listening."

He closed his eyes and relaxed into the water, smiling as he listened to her talk. He had his baby back.

Finally.

Johnson Family

Check out the Brooks family cousins in the Johnson Family series!

For nine years Ivy Johnson hid her daughter's paternity. When Lucas Baylor discovers the truth, will he be able to forgive her deception? And how will Ivy ever protect her heart? Find out in Unforgettable, Book 1.

CEO Cyrus Johnson is rich, powerful, and used to getting his way. His estranged wife Daniella Barrett-Johnson wants a divorce. Will he give it to her, or will he find a way to bind her to him for good? Read Perfect, Book 2 to find out.

Trenton Johnson and Alannah Bailey have been best friends since they were kids. Dare they risk their friendship for a chance at love? Get the answer in Just Friends, Book 3.

Gavin Johnson and Terri Slade immediately heat up the sheets, but once Terri breaks her relationship rules for Gavin, will his inner demons cause their relationship to fall apart? Find out in The Rules, Book 4.

For years, Xavier Johnson has been known as "the good one." Yet because of his strong feelings for Diana Cambridge, he demonstrates that he also has a bad side. Find out how bad he can be in Good Behavior, Book 5.

* * *

Audiobook samples and free short stories available at www.delaneydiamond.com.

ALSO BY DELANEY DIAMOND

Check out the other books in the Brooks Family series and get to know the other family members!

Simone Brooks meets and falls in love with nightclub owner Cameron Bennett, but will her wealth and status drive a wedge between them? Find out in A Passionate Love.

Can a sudden, single kiss get Oscar Brooks and Sylvie Johnson back together after fifteen years apart? Read about their reconciliation in Passion Rekindled.

After a scary break-in at her apartment, will Ella Brooks find love in an unexpected place, the second time around with Detective Tyrone Evers? Follow their romantic journey in Do Over.

Malik Brooks is celibate. Can he resist the fireworks between him and relationship expert Lindsay Winthrop when they enter into a fake relationship? Read their funny, sexy path to love in Wild Thoughts.

Bad boy Stephan Brooks is willing to risk it all for fashion director Roselle Parker. Find out why in Two Nights in Paris.

The biggest mistake Reese Brooks ever made was hurting the woman he loved. Will he ever be able to win Nina Winthrop's love again? Or is it too little too late? Read their story in Deeper Than Love.

ABOUT THE AUTHOR

Delaney Diamond is the USA Today Bestselling Author of sweet, sensual, passionate romance novels. Originally from the U.S. Virgin Islands, she now lives in Atlanta, Georgia. She reads romance novels, mysteries, thrillers, and a fair amount of nonfiction. When she's not busy reading or writing, she's in the kitchen trying out new recipes, dining at one of her favorite restaurants, or traveling to an interesting locale.

Enjoy free reads and the first chapter of all her novels on her website. Join her mailing list to get sneak peeks, notices of sale prices, and find out about new releases.

Join her mailing list
www.delaneydiamond.com

facebook.com/DelaneyDiamond
twitter.com/DelaneyDiamond
bookbub.com/authors/delaney-diamond
pinterest.com/delaneydiamond

Made in the USA
Monee, IL
02 April 2022